A feeling of menace hung in the air

The unreal silence on the mountainside puzzled Claire as she skied along beside Dave Heron. Suddenly she turned and saw an enormous overhang of snow break loose in the bright, melting sunlight.

"Hurry!" Dave shouted. They launched themselves down the hill in a mad dash. Behind them the avalanche of snow and rock rumbled and threatened.

Claire looked back and saw a cascading rush of whiteness almost on top of them. The last thing she glimpsed was a flash of blue sky before she was buried in a cold, silent world.

Other

MYSTIQUE BOOKS

by DENISE NOEL

For a free catalogue listing all available Mystique Books, send your name and address to:

MYSTIQUE BOOKS,
M.P.O. Box 707, Niagara Falls, N.Y. 14302
In Canada: 649 Ontario St., Stratford, Ontario N5A 6W2

Blind
Obsession

by DENISE NOEL

MYSTIQUE BOOKS

TORONTO · LONDON · NEW YORK

BLIND OBSESSION/first published March 1980

ISBN 0-373-50070-X

PRINTED IN U.S.A.

Chapter 1

The wind lashed at the small car with increasing fury. Ever since leaving the precarious shelter of the streets of Chartres, southwest of Paris, the car had become more and more vulnerable to the onslaught of the worsening storm.

Her eyes fixed straight ahead, the young woman clenched the steering wheel, guiding the car through the black night, scarcely aided by the glow of the headlights. She bit her lip in frustration; the pounding rain was the latest in a series of events thwarting her escape. First, there had been fog, then a howling wind to impede her progress; now it was a slashing, driving rain that showed no sign of letting up. *I've got this far*, she thought determinedly. *I'm certainly not going to give up now.*

She had deliberately gone out of her way to send a telegram from a city south of Paris in order to mislead those who might think of pursuing her. The detour had cost her four hours and now, with the storm, she would have to drive all night to reach her destination,

Brittany, in the northwest of France. Only in Brittany could she find the peace and tranquility she so desperately sought.

She searched through the rain for some sign post to give her an indication of how far she'd traveled but saw none. Come to think of it, she hadn't seen any since she came onto this road after making her detour. Maybe she should check her map just to be sure. She pulled off the road and turned off the ignition.

Nervously, she began to unfold the road map and reached up to switch on the overhead light. The woods on either side of the road were not familiar, and as the road itself revealed no familiar signs, she studied the map in an effort to see where she'd gone wrong. She saw her error and figured that by continuing straight ahead for eight or so miles, she would be able to get back on the road to Louville. From there she could head straight to Brittany.

She started the engine and stepped on the accelerator, and the car shot back onto the road. Suddenly there was a muffled explosion, and the next instant, the steering wheel swung crazily through her hands. Gripping it until her knuckles were white, she slowly decreased her speed, using all her strength to keep the car on the road.

The ghostly shadow of a huge tree loomed in the beam of the headlights, disappeared, only to be replaced by another, even closer . . . then the road again, bumpy and winding. The car gradually lost speed and finally lurched to a halt, broadside across the road.

Fighting back tears, her nerves frayed from tension, the young woman got out of the car to look at the shredded tire. A gust of wind blew rain in her face and whipped her golden hair into her eyes.

The car stood right across the middle of the road, effectively blocking any traffic that might be coming from either direction. The tire lay in pieces alongside. She would have to find the jack and put on the spare. Covering her face with her hands, she let the tears run freely down her cheeks. Her knees buckled and she leaned against the side of the car sobbing.

Pulling herself together, finally, she opened the trunk and felt around for the tools she would need. She found the tire arm and began, clumsily, to loosen the nuts on the wheel. She was just wrestling with the second nut when a sound caught her attention above the howling wind. Was it a car? No, perhaps not; in the gale, she was imagining things.

Just then, out of the gloom flashed a pair of blinding headlights. She watched dazedly, rooted to the spot, as the car slowed and finally stopped beside her own.

A tall young man in his late twenties, casually dressed in corduroy trousers and a tweed jacket, got out of the car and came toward her. He had thick black, curly hair, and dark brown eyes, a little like her own. His face, however, was clouded with irritation.

She opened her mouth to begin her explanation as to why her car was in the middle of the road, but found herself unable to say a word. She lifted her hand to brush her hair away from her face, and realized to her horror, that it was trembling.

She tried again "I . . . I had a flat tire and . . . and nearly ran into a tree. I'm . . . I'm sorry. . . ."

The man's look softened, but he continued to look at her intently, quizzically, as though searching for something, while he spoke. "That must have been frightening for you. Perhaps I can help . . . but the first thing we have to do is get both cars out of the middle of the road, in case some other poor unfortunate driver...."

While she muttered incoherent thanks, he got into her car and slowly drove it onto the side of the road, then did the same with his, shining his lights onto the damaged wheel.

While he changed the tire he commented conversationally on the weather and the hazards of night driving. Was he giving her a chance to calm herself, she wondered. Did he think it at all strange that she was so distraught over a simple flat tire she didn't think to move her car off the road, or did he realize that there was more—much more—to account for her nervous state? She felt panic rising again, and only with a supreme effort did she manage to quell it.

"Are you going far, Miss, er—"

"Severac. Francine Severac."

A frown wrinkled the man's brow for a second then disappeared. "How do you do? I'm David Heron. The spare's on now, but I suggest you get another tire at the first opportunity. This one's no good to you now," he said kicking the remnants of the blown tire. Suddenly, as if just noticing how wet she was, he added solicitously, "Forgive me, Miss Severac, I should have insisted you stay inside your car. But perhaps I can make amends. May I offer you a warm bed for the night at the home of a friend of mine? I was on my way there just now. I call her Aunt Suzanne, though she's no relation. She's the aunt of a good friend of mine, and like a second mother to me. Well, Miss... Severac?"

Her first inclination was to refuse immediately; she must keep going, put more distance between herself and.... But, even as she thought that, she realized how bone weary she was, and realized that it might be dangerous for her to drive much farther without getting a night's rest. "That's very kind of you," she finally stammered, "but isn't there a hotel somewhere reasonably near?"

"Well, yes, a small one. But I assure you, Aunt Suzanne would never forgive me if I didn't bring you back with me. She'll be delighted to see you—she loves having guests. She says it keeps her young. So you'll follow me in your car? It's only seven or eight miles from here."

"All right, thank you . . . if you're sure I won't be in the way. . . ."

As she got back into her car, her eyes fell on the leather case, lying open, containing her driver's license and insurance. Her eyes widened in horror as she realized that David Heron could easily have read the information on the license when he got into her car to drive it to the side of the road. She looked at the incriminating piece of paper, and the name that seemed to jump out at her: Claire de Montebourg. He must have read it! No wonder he had looked so puzzled when she'd introduced herself as Francine Severac. In fact it was the name of an old school friend—the first name that had sprung into her mind when he'd asked her name. What must he have thought? Would he question her about it . . . or worse, make inquiries about her, perhaps to the police? Her panic welling up again, she began to follow the taillights already receding into the blackness ahead of her.

Chapter 2

Some twenty minutes later, the two cars turned into the driveway and stopped in front of a fairly large farmhouse. It was too dark to see more than the outline of the house, and by this time Claire was so totally exhausted, she wouldn't have cared if it had been a barn—all she needed was somewhere to lie down. Perhaps she might even manage to sleep, although she doubted it.

Dave handed her out of her car, got her suitcase out of the trunk and rang the front door bell. Almost immediately the front door was opened by a smiling, uniformed maid. Just behind her was a gray-haired, middle-aged lady, coming toward them with a warm, welcoming smile and outstretched arms. "David, you're here at last! Peter and I were beginning to wonder where you'd got to! And Simon refused to go to bed until you arrived. Oh, you've brought a guest—how lovely!"

"Hello, Aunt Suzanne. Yes, I have brought a guest," David Heron replied with a smile. "I'd like to introduce you to . . . Francine Severac. Francine, I'd like you to meet Mrs. Suzanne Chanoy, affectionately known by one and all as Aunt Suzanne. I'd also like you to meet Marie, Aunt Suzanne's right hand, who's been here as long as any of us can remember." The maid smiled shyly, then departed quietly with the small suitcases David had removed from both cars.

The introductions over, David Heron proceeded to give Suzanne Chanoy a quick account of what had happened.

"Oh, you poor dear!" clucked Aunt Suzanne sympathetically, surveying Claire's bedraggled state. "You must be frozen. Your clothes are soaking wet! I'll bet you're hungry, too. I'll ask Marie to run a hot bath for you. The spare room at the corner is always made up, so you're quite welcome to make yourself at home tonight."

Claire started to protest but was cut short by Aunt Suzanne's firm voice. "No, I won't hear of your staying anywhere else tonight. You look exhausted and very pale. While you're having your bath, I'll heat up some soup for you; would you like that?"

"Thank you very much, Mrs. Chanoy; you're being very kind," Claire replied weakly. The thought of a hot bath and something to eat was irresistible.

A door opened into the hallway, and a young man, about the same age as David Heron, appeared holding a little boy by the hand. "Hello, Dave," he smiled. "You're late. . . ."

"Hi, Peter, and hi Simon-who-should-have-been-in-bed-ages-ago! I'd like you both to meet Francine Severac. Francine, meet Peter Breveley, a great pal of mine and his young brother, Simon. Both bona fide nephews of Aunt Suzanne!

"I'm late, Pete, because I helped Francine change her flat tire on the road a few miles back." Claire smiled at David's tactful description of the incident, and reminded herself that it was a mixed blessing that he happened to be passing by.

A WARM SCENTED BATH did much to restore Claire's physical state, although her mind whirled around in a frenzy. These people had been very kind . . . but if they only knew!

Pulling out a pair of wool trousers and a thick sweater from her suitcase, she quickly redressed, even though every muscle in her body ached, and went downstairs to join the others.

Aunt Suzanne met her in the hall and led her into the library, where Peter was sitting finishing his after-dinner coffee. Simon, his thin, pale face intent, was busy lining up toy racing cars on the carpet.

As Claire walked into the room she looked around, noting how very different it was from the cold, elegant rooms of her parents' château. The furniture was hopelessly mismatched, nonetheless Suzanne Chanoy had somehow managed to make the room cozy and attractive.

"Now dear, I'll go and heat up that soup—and please call me Aunt Suzanne; everybody does and it's so much less formal than Mrs. Chanoy." With that, Aunt Suzanne disappeared, shutting the library door behind her.

"You're probably very confused with the setup in this house." Peter smiled sympathetically. "Perhaps I can simplify things for you a bit. The little tyke there—" he pointed to Simon "—lives here with Aunt Suzanne." Lowering his voice, he continued, "He's got a strange illness, and my father thought the country air out here might help. Extensive testing has been done . . . but we can't find anything. He won't eat, and as you can see, he's far too thin—almost literally wasting away. He gets vitamin injections, of course, but he needs to fill out a whole lot more.

"Anyway," Peter continued, realizing that he'd digressed, "when my mother died—when Simon was born—Aunt Suzanne at once suggested that he come to live here . . . and Simon's very happy except that he's still not eating. Aunt Suzanne's tried everything, but nothing's worked so far. Even surrounded by doctors, the poor little kid keeps on getting thinner and thinner."

"Surrounded by doctors?" echoed Claire, her heart beginning to race.

"Yes. I'm one, Dave's one, and my father is one—you might even have heared of him. Dr. Andrew Breveley: he's quite a well-known neurosurgeon."

"No . . . I haven't. . . ."

"Well, no reason you should have, I guess. It's just that he's been in the papers recently; he developed a new brain-surgery technique. Anyway, enough of that. Dave may have mentioned that he and I share an apartment in Paris. We try and come out here as often as we can, though: good food and good company!"

"Mrs. Chanoy—Aunt Suzanne—has no children of her own?"

Peter shook his head. "No, no children, but she treats Simon like her own child."

Peter stopped talking and seemed to withdraw into his memories. Suddenly, Claire felt very lonely, and had to struggle not to release the tears of self-pity that were welling up in her eyes. There was so much love in this house, she thought. Everyone truly seemed to care about everyone else. She looked at Simon. Yes, he was very thin and fragile-looking, but he seemed to have a happy nature and appeared very secure in the blanket of Aunt Suzanne's love.

As if her looking at Simon triggered a reaction from Peter, he said, "Simon, my friend, it's time for you to go to bed."

"Already? Will you come up later to tuck me in?"

"Yes, and I'll be up, too, love; now off you go." Aunt Suzanne had overheard the last bit of the conversation as she came into the library carrying a tray with a steaming bowl of soup and a plate of bread and cheese. She rang for Marie to come and collect Simon who was slowly packing up his cars.

Giving the tray to Claire, Aunt Suzanne settled herself in a comfortable armchair beside Peter. Just as she was picking up the petit point she was working on, the library door opened, and Dave came in, his hair still wet from the shower.

He sank onto the sofa with a sigh. "I just saw Simon being carted off to bed. He still isn't gaining any weight is he?"

"You can't expect him to gain weight as long as he keeps eating like a bird," said Aunt Suzanne. "There must be some way of getting him to eat more. I wonder if a holiday in the mountains would do him any good."

"That's certainly worth considering," Dave replied. "I was also thinking perhaps some sea air might do the trick."

"Well, no point of thinking about it right now," Aunt Suzanne said matter-of-factly. "We're not budging an inch till it warms up a bit. She heaved herself out of the armchair. Shall we go up and say goodnight to Simon now?" she asked, then turned to Claire. "Will you join us, my dear?"

"I saw a piano in the living room," Claire began shyly. "Would you mind very much if I played it for a few minutes before I went to bed?"

Aunt Suzanne started, and visibly paled. "Of course . . . my dear. It hasn't been played for a while. It would be nice to have a little music in the house."

Dave turned to her. "Aunt Suzanne, are you sure. . . ."

"Quite sure, David, thank you. I was just a little surprised that's all. It's at times like this that all the memories come flooding back. . . . They are similar in many ways, Miss Severac . : . and Margaret. Let's just hope that your friend's fate is not the same as my daughter's. . . ."

Chapter 3

Claire woke with a start, her heart pounding. Where was she? What had happened? It was pitch-black; she fumbled for the bedside light and turned it on. For a moment she lay there, staring at the totally unfamiliar surroundings, before she remembered the events of the day before.

Surprisingly she had slept quite well in the old-fashioned heavy oak bed. The serenity and loving atmosphere of the house had pervaded her senses, lulling her momentarily into calmness. But now she was awake, and it was time to face the world again. She must get to Brittany today, where she could stay undiscovered and try to find some peace for herself.

Looking at her watch, she realized it would soon be dawn. The rest of the household was sleeping, and she could escape and be on her way without anyone questioning her.

She got out of bed and dressed quietly and hurriedly. Finding some notepaper in the desk under the window, she sat down and wrote a note to Aunt

Suzanne, thanking her for her hospitality and all her kindness. Then, taking her shoes and her suitcase in her hand, she crept down the darkened stairway and out the front door.

Dawn was just breaking, the skies had cleared a little, but it was going to be another cold day.

Claire sat in her car, waiting for the engine to warm up, and looked up at the old, comfortable house. How wonderful it must be to live like those kind people wrapped in loving support; how much easier it would be to face life's problems!

Sighing, she drove quietly down the driveway and onto the road. Then she remembered the telegram she had sent off the night before to throw her pursuers off her track. It should have got there by now. . . .

IN AN OPULENT CHATEAU in the fashionable Paris suburb of Neuilly, a distinguished-looking, if severe, gray-haired man was finishing his second cup of coffee while the maid began to clear away the breakfast dishes. As he began reading the last page of the newspaper, he heard the butler come into the dining room and looked up to see what he wanted.

"A telegram, m'lord."

"Thank you, James. Has Miss Claire come in yet?"

"No, m'lord. Her car is not in the courtyard." Seeing that the count had no further questions, nor, apparently, any more need of him, the butler quietly withdrew.

The Count de Montebourg looked at the telegram and his hand trembled as he picked up the ivory letter opener. Hadn't he done precisely the same thing before, many years ago? He wondered if, even now, his heart was sufficiently protected from hurt by the shield he had so carefully built around himself over the years.

He opened the envelope and the words of the telegram swam before his eyes. Covering his face with one hand, he summoned all his self-control to remain calm and prevent old memories from creeping into his mind. A minute or two later, he read the telegram. His face expressing a mixture of anger and concern, he strode over to his desk and picked up the telephone.

As he was reading the cable a second time he was joined by Elaine, his second wife. Tall, extremely thin, and elegantly dressed, Elaine carried herself as a beautiful woman should. Yet, though she paid great attention to her appearance, her face, with its downward lines and pinched mouth, betrayed a certain cold hardness. After reading the telegram her husband wordlessly held out to her, she subsided into a chair with a small groan.

Elaine read the message again, this time out loud.

"Have decided to leave for good. Going to Oliver. Sorry to cause you grief but could not bear listen what you would say. Will always think of you father, love Claire."

So, she thought to herself, despite all their efforts, his emotional daughter was once again doing exactly as she pleased, with no thought for anyone else. But this time . . . !

"Richard, we—"

"Please, my dear," interrupted the count, recognizing the signs of anger in his wife's expression, "calm yourself. We have to think of what's to be done."

"I don't know what to do! She's never been anything else but difficult with me. Haven't I tried to look after her as though she were my very own daughter? Didn't she always have the very best nurses and nannies? And what does she do in return? She's always been the most ungrateful child. Have you ever known her to be anything but secretive and uncommunicative?"

"Yes...I remember a time when she was very different," replied the count, softly.

Elaine shot him an astonished look. Leaning back in her chair, she closed her eyes and her face took on an expression of weariness and long-suffering. She considered people who were demonstrative to be ridiculous, and she thought any manifestation of tenderness was nothing short of vulgarity.

The count walked over to the mantelpiece and leaned against it. He ran his hand through his still plentiful iron-gray hair, contemplating the portrait on the wall opposite. It was of a little girl smiling shyly, dressed in a yellow smocked dress, a matching ribbon tying back her long hair: a portrait of Claire at the age of eight.

"I know that you did your best with her, Elaine," he said. "But the fact remains that we didn't manage to give her what she needed, which was a climate of confidence in herself and her surroundings. Unfortunately, now that I realize that, it's too late."

"You have no reason to blame yourself; Claire was always a difficult child."

"Difficult, perhaps, but very intelligent, too. She always did so well at school, and I never showed her how pleased I was. The same can be said of her record at college. She has done extremely well in her law studies, and I am well aware that I have never once let her know how proud I was of her."

"Proud? But you always said that all of those diplomas and achievements were utterly useless because she'd never have to work for a living!"

"Yes, but I was wrong. For some, work is a necessity, but for others, it is essential as a means of expressing themselves."

"Yes, yes, all right. But what do we do now? We're being forced to accept her marriage to this Oliver person."

The count went over to where his wife was seated. His eyes had suddenly become like pinpoints of steel in his strong face. His tone was cutting. "You know as well as I do that this wedding cannot take place! Elaine, I want the truth: what did you say to Claire to make her take off so suddenly?"

The woman flushed, then paled. "It's not what you think!" she protested. "The girl was madly in love with Oliver and thought that you would be against the match, so she decided to go ahead and present us with a fait accompli, it seems!"

"But Claire didn't go to Oliver."

"What?"

"I called Oliver's house just before you came down," continued the count in the same biting tone. "Oliver left for Naples last week; I spoke to his sister. She did tell me one thing, though: Claire had broken off with Oliver before he left!"

The countess stood up, obviously upset. "That makes things even more serious! Where could she have gone? She must be found at once! Where was the telegram sent from? We must notify the police quickly!"

"And have her picked up and brought back here in a police car? You're not thinking straight, my dear. I still want to know what happened to make her run off like this. What did you say to her?"

"Nothing! I swear it, nothing at all! I didn't even mention that you were planning to have a talk with her. I don't think I even saw her yesterday . . . yes, I did. Now I remember, she wanted me to fire my maid . . . for no reason at all. Claire was in a terrible temper. I tried to calm her, but she flounced out of my room, and that's the last I saw of her. It's true, you must believe me!"

The count merely looked at her. She seemed sincere, he had no reason to doubt her. Claire's sudden departure would mean a lot of upset and bad publicity, and Elaine would never have done anything to precipitate such a state of affairs. He knew her horror of what she termed sensationalism.

He leaned back in his chair. Memories ran haphazardly through his mind. He remembered when Claire was a child—the quiet contentedness of those first years, then the tragedy that seemed to put an end to their happiness. He realized that he had not become nearly as tough and hard as he had imagined. Claire's leaving had affected him far more than he was prepared to admit.

"There won't be any publicity or scandal about 'runaways', or an impromptu marriage," he said. "I'll see to it that her leaving home will appear quite natural. There's no need for you to worry about headlines in the papers."

"I doubt that she has any money with her," Elaine remarked matter-of-factly. "How's she going to live?"

"I think she'll manage, somehow. I gave her quite a large amount of money recently for her Christmas holidays, so she's not quite penniless for the time being. Maybe she had to get away to assert her independence from us. We'll just have to wait awhile and see what happens."

As he was speaking, the count's face had resumed its customary expression of aloofness. He walked over to his wife, lifted her finely-boned, well-manicured hand, and kissed it.

Elaine was reassured. Feeling free of all suspicion, she left the room quite happy and more than contented that her stepdaughter had really left home. She hoped Claire would stay away; Elaine only found her presence irritating.

Chapter 4

Claire drove as fast as she dared. There had been another heavy rain shower, and the roads were slick. While she concentrated on her driving, another part of her mind was flickering over the events of the past twenty-four hours.

She thought about David Heron. She recalled how he'd often looked at her, a quizzical expression on his face. She wondered whether her abrupt departure from Milhouse would increase his curiosity about her Did he suspect something? Had he guessed? He never questioned her about not telling him her correct name.

Claire shrugged. Idle conjecture was a waste of time. Her mind would be put to more constructive use, she thought, if she gave some attention to what she would do—not only once she got to Brittany—but in the long-term future, as well.

But her thoughts continued to dwell on the recent events of the day before. Obsessively, though vaguely, a single fugitive thought kept darting around in her head. It was something unpleasant, she knew.

Something that had come to the surface of her mind
just before she had awoken in the morning. She could
still feel the panicky feeling it had created. She tried to
organize her thoughts and capture the fleeting memory. Suddenly, everything became quite clear.

It wasn't David Heron's curiosity about her true
identity that she needed to worry about. It was the fact
that he was a doctor. And Peter, too. Wasn't it a
doctor's business to diagnose illness? Hers must have
been plain to see, both in her eyes and in the irrational
way she behaved.

Mad! The terrible syllable resounded in her mind.
Yes, she was insane . . . and any attempt she might
make to escape would be utterly futile. No matter
where she went, what she did, she could imagine the
outcome—in months? Years? With the passing of each
successive day, she would become more disoriented,
more unable to cope with everyday life.

A pale sun filtered through the bare branches of the
trees lining the road. She stopped the car, got out and
stretched. She walked to a tree stump and sat down,
trying to sort out and calm her thoughts.

The air was mild, the sun had a little warmth in it,
and the area was sheltered. The birds, momentarily
silenced by the slamming of the car door, resumed
their singing. Claire watched a large blackbird who
seemed to be conducting the morning concert. The
scene took her back to the family mansion in Neuilly,
on the outskirts of Paris, which she had left . . . was it
only the day before? She closed her eyes. The memory
of yesterday came back, with one incident particularly
clear. . . .

She had woken up early, looking forward to having

breakfast alone with her father. Elaine, she knew, wouldn't be down until much later. There were only a few days left of her Christmas break, then she would have to return to her law studies at the university.

Claire sang while she dressed. When she got down to the dining room, her father was just finishing his breakfast.

Claire was happy to have the opportunity to spend time alone with her father, although her great affection for him was composed of a mixture of tenderness and fear. She had the greatest admiration for the tall, distinguished man, but she had always had to try so hard to please him—to win his approval of everything she did. Sometimes, she would think that she had noticed a spark of interest in her doings, but his cool, dry voice would soon dispel the illusion.

She walked over to him and kissed his cheek.

"You seem to be in a very good mood this morning," he said, as he looked at her. "What are your plans for the day?"

"Nothing special. I had thought of going to the library but it's turned out to be such a nice day that I might put it off until another time. I'd rather go riding in the Bois de Boulogne; the weather is ideal for it."

Jeanne, who began clearing away the count's breakfast dishes, was taking her time about it, obviously in order to eavesdrop on the conversation. Her sly face averted, she moved as slowly as she could, rearranging dishes on the buffet.

"Perhaps I'll call Oliver and ask him to join me," Claire continued.

At the mention of Oliver's name, the count's face darkened.

"Come and see me in my study as soon as you've finished your breakfast," the count said, rising from the table. "I want to talk to you about something."

He picked up his newspaper and walked out of the room.

Immediately, Claire's joy in the beautiful day vanished. Her heart began to beat more quickly as she began to wonder what had caused the "summons." The count's expression had been formidable when he left the room. But at least one thought cheered her up: Elaine was still upstairs and wouldn't be there to make matters worse. Over the years, Claire had tried to like her stepmother, but Elaine's obvious dislike and contempt for Claire had made this impossible. She sighed.

Finishing her tea, she headed down the hall. In the large study, her father stood waiting, looking out into the garden. The count seemed to be staring intently, but when he turned slightly, Claire saw that his eyes were glazed, his thoughts had taken him miles away.

He turned and came toward her.

"You wanted to talk to me, father?"

"Come and sit down," he said, gently taking her by the arm and leading her over to a sunny corner of the room. Claire's face, lit by the morning sun, was quite lovely. The count looked at her for a moment, frowned, and then went on. "Tell me, Claire, is this thing with Oliver all that serious?"

"Yes, father, it couldn't be more serious. I'm afraid that's something you're just going to have to get used to."

"Come now, is Oliver really any more to you than a tennis partner and someone to go riding with?"

"We've talked about getting married."

The count made a visible effort to remain calm, but Claire saw the anger in his eyes. She braced herself for the outburst.

"It may be fashionable among your student friends to let their parents know they are engaged as a fait accompli, but in this family I will not tolerate such a thing. I must say that I find your attitude somewhat offensive."

"Father," asked Claire, patiently, "if Oliver were to come here and ask for my hand in marriage, would you even see him?"

"Never!" replied the count vehemently. "And you know that as well as I do."

"Then, if you won't see him, how can I present anything other than a 'fait accompli' as you call it? What on earth have you got against Oliver?" Claire rushed on. "He's rich, titled, intelligent and very attractive. Why don't you like him?"

"For one thing, he's much too old for you. He's sixteen years your senior and that's almost a whole generation! And I've heard some of the stories going around about his behavior. Elaine has talked to you about this often enough, but you're just too stubborn to listen!"

"Elaine doesn't approve of a single thing I do," Claire answered with a trace of bitterness. "And you know that as well as I do!"

For a moment the count looked at his daughter in silence, fixing her with his flat, icy stare.

"I think it would be better if we were to say no more about this matter," he said finally. "As your father, I feel it is my duty to tell you that, in my opinion, your thinking of marrying Oliver is nothing but childish nonsense. If you persist in this behavior, it will have to be against my express wishes."

Claire rose to her feet. "I'm twenty years old, father," she said defiantly. "And I'm quite old enough to be married, regardless of what you think."

She could hardly contain her anger. She had told her father more than she had intended. True, Oliver and she had idly discussed marriage, and ever since, it had occurred to her with increasing force that it would be an ideal way to escape the hostile atmosphere of the château where nothing she did was met with approval. Yes, she would marry Oliver! Furious, she headed for the door.

"Claire!"

The slightest hint of supplication in her father's voice made her stop and turn around.

"Claire, instead of losing your temper, try to stop for a moment and really think about this step. You won't find your happiness with this man. And...I have something to tell you which is very important to all of us. When you've heard it, you can make up your own mind about marrying Oliver. Now, I'm going to ask you not to see him for at least five days. You know what terrible anniversary that day is for us. We'll talk again then. After I've told you what I have to say, you'll be completely free to make your own decision about marrying Oliver. But in the meantime, I want your promise that you won't see him."

"Very well, father," answered Claire, more moved by her father's words than she cared to show. "You have my word."

That afternoon Claire sat in her room, writing to Oliver. When she had finished, she realized that it had started to rain, and a gray pall seemed to surround the room. She picked up a book and walked through the silent house up to the third floor.

She entered the small bright room overlooking the beautiful Bois de Boulogne. This had been her old nursery; Claire still thought of it as a kind of hideaway and used it to store books and magazines she wanted to keep. One entire wall was covered with memorabilia of her younger days.

She sat down in a wicker rocking chair and began to read. A few minutes later, her reading was interrupted by the sound of voices, which echoed quite clearly in the room.

She looked up. One of the sliding doors to the closet was slightly ajar. The back wall of the closet was the partition between the nursery and a linen closet on the other side.

Not wishing to eavesdrop on other people's conversation, even inadvertently, she got up to close the closet door, but the first words that reached her ears clearly caused her to freeze.

She recognized the voices of Jeanne, the maid, and Mrs. Martineau, a former chambermaid that the family had kept on as a laundry woman. She was an old woman, whose sole remaining pleasure in life was picking up and relating, with suitable embellishments, any tidbit of gossip she could find.

"And I'm telling you that she'll never marry that Oliver de Vere! Her father would never approve! They were having quite an argument this morning. Too bad they weren't talking in the dining room. I couldn't hear a word they said in the study. I do wish I could have heard what the old man said to her!"

"Oh, I would have loved to have been there, if only

to see the expression on that spoiled brat's face!"
added Mrs. Martineau, with relish.

Claire felt the impact of the words as though she had
been slapped.

"Oh, she's spoiled all right! Do you remember the
tantrums she used to have as a child? If I'd had
anything to do with it, she'd have felt the back of my
hand more than once, I can tell you!"

"Yes, I agree. But she'd have only gone running to
her father and told him, and that wouldn't have done
either of us any good—we'd have been out of this
house so fast, it would have made our heads spin! But
back to her marrying Mr. de Vere: I doubt she'll marry
him, or anyone for that matter. Illnesses like hers don't
show up until after a person's properly grown up—
and then they are passed on to the children!"

"Well, I don't know about that. I think Miss Claire's
madness will just suddenly blow up one day, and
fairly soon. Have you ever really looked at her eyes?
Already, there's something more than a bit strange
there. You were here, weren't you, Mrs. Martineau,
when her mother killed herself?"

The words stunned Claire. Suddenly trembling
from head to foot, she clung to the door. She'd always
been told that her mother had died in an accident!
Gasping for breath, she strained to hear the next
words.

"Yes, I was here. They kept saying it was an
accident, but who in their right mind would go for a
swim in a pond in December! Well, I ask you! I was
told, and I believe it, that water always held a very
strange attraction for her, just as it did for her
mother and her grandmother. She was a neurotic
and unstable as they come. You know the count

took her to Switzerland for a change of scenery. They were there for four years, in total, and that was where Claire was born. I came to work for them after they got back. And a year later, the countess threw herself into the pond. You can't escape your destiny, you know. . . ."

The former chambermaid went on as though she were a great authority on the subject of mental disorders.

"The sickness is in their blood. In this family, cousins have been marrying one another for generations. It's well known that that causes the brain to go all queer after a time."

They must have finished putting away the laundry because there was a sound of a door being closed, and then the voices could no longer be heard.

Claire felt her knees getting weak. Her forehead was damp, and the room spun round before her eyes. She sat down abruptly, her head on her knees.

When she felt better, the house was still and silent. Suffering from a sudden fierce attack of migraine, Claire walked slowly downstairs to her room, the thick, crimson carpet muffling the sound of her footsteps. The door to her room was half-open. She pushed it, and her eyes widened in astonishment.

"What do you think you're doing?"

Leaning toward the light to see better, Jeanne was avidly reading the note that Claire had written to Oliver a little while earlier. She looked up, flushing, then threw the note onto the desk, giving a little laugh.

"Get out this instant!" said Claire, her voice rising in anger. After what she had heard in the nursery, her self-control nearly snapped. Sensing this, Jeanne half ran out of the room.

Later that afternoon, Elaine arrived home from the gallery. She was in a foul temper, she had been caught in the rain, and had been unable to get a taxi for ages. She was also very tired, and had retired to her bedroom for a short rest before dinner. She had hardly put her head down on the pillow when there was an urgent knock on the door.

"Come in . . . oh, it's you, Claire." Her tone made it obvious that her stepdaughter's visit was anything but welcome. "What is it? You know that I have to rest after one of these functions. What a crowd! But the exhibition was absolutely marvelous."

"Forgive me for interrupting," said Claire in a tight, controlled voice. "But I have something I have to talk to you about."

"Can't it wait, for heaven's sake?" Then, seeing the anger on Claire's face, Elaine sat up, massaging her temples lightly with her long red-tipped fingers. "All right, what is it?"

"Jeanne must be fired."

Elaine was suddenly wide awake. "What? You can't be serious."

"On the contrary, I'm quite serious. A short while ago I caught Jeanne in my room, reading a letter I'd just finished writing. I was furious and told her to get out immediately."

"First, you're rude to my maid and now you want me to fire her! You don't know what you're talking about! I've put up with a lot of nonsense from you, but this time, you've gone too far."

"Jeanne is indiscreet and totally untrustworthy! She cannot be allowed to stay on here!"

Elaine looked up at Claire, whose body was still

rigid with anger. "Was your desk locked, or was the letter lying around untidily, open for anyone to see?"

Claire was becoming exasperated. "What difference does it make? She had it in her hand and was reading it! It was none of her business, and she has no right to go through my belongings."

"Really, Claire, your arrogance is beyond all reason," replied Elaine in a bored tone of voice. "Next time, try to remember to put your things away. Now would you please allow me to get a minute or two of rest before dinner?"

"Jeanne has to be fired," Claire insisted. "I don't want to see her in this house again. I'll see that it's done, even if I have to do it myself."

"And what makes you think you have the right to do any such thing?" Elaine replied superciliously. "From now on, you are expressly forbidden to give orders of any kind to any of the servants. If you want to order servants around and fire them at your slightest whim, you're going to have to wait until you have your own household."

Then she looked at her stepdaughter and her expression changed to one of mock pity, as she lowered her voice and said sweetly, "That is, my dear, if the time should ever come when you are able to maintain a house of your own."

This was the real Elaine, unveiled. The hypocritical smile, the scathing tone, the venomous intent were all so much a part of Elaine that it took a few seconds for Claire to fully understand the meaning of what she had just heard. Realization brought a slump to her shoulders, and she turned on her heel and walked out of the room.

Now she knew what her father had to tell her. Well, she could at least spare him the embarrassment of having to make so difficult a declaration.

She would escape from this house, where everyone was watching and waiting for her to go insane.

Chapter 5

Claire had just driven through Rennes; she had about a hundred miles still to go. The small village where Anne-Marie lived seemed very far away, even though she had already begun to drive into familiar territory. Soon she would reach the haven of her nanny's arms. Until now, Claire hadn't fully realized how much she missed her.

Anne-Marie Leduc had also been nanny to Claire's mother. The passing years had done nothing to diminish their affection for one another, and upon her return from Switzerland, Claire's mother had called Anne-Marie back to look after her baby girl, Claire.

Eight years later, Elaine, newly married to the count, had fired Anne-Marie. She had announced that Claire needed a proper, licensed nanny, and that this woman, whose common-sense approach had worked wonders in building the confidence of the little girl, was simply not qualified to bring up her stepdaughter. Claire's tears and endless pleading had been in vain. She never forgot the wrenching pain of nanny's departure, and from that day on, it seemed, her relationship with her stepmother began to deteriorate.

In order to keep in touch with her much-loved nanny, Claire had got Anne-Marie's address from the old gardener, who had been only too happy to do whatever he could to help. Since then, with the old man's help, a loving stream of letters had been flowing regularly between the small Brittany town of St. Quay Portrieux and the lonely château in Neuilly. For two years, Claire had even been able to spend holidays with her beloved nanny without her parents' knowledge. She managed to get herself invited to spend the time with Francine Severac, a schoolfriend, whose parents had a summer house nearby. Mrs. Severac, who was very much aware of Claire's misery, willingly allowed the two friends to stay with Anne-Marie for weeks at a time.

Those times were among Claire's fondest memories. Now, once again she would have the peace and happiness of those childhood holidays. She began to look forward eagerly to her arrival at Anne-Marie's little cottage. She hadn't had time to let her know she was coming, but the one sure thing in her turbulent life at the moment was the warm welcome she would receive from her nanny.

Claire, a smile on her face, began to visualize the cozy little house. She remembered that it was always spotlessly clean—nanny was forever whisking away imaginary dust, and polishing the pieces of brass and copper, so that they never failed to sparkle brightly in the sun or firelight. Claire remembered the ivory elephant, taking a place of pride on a small table between the two windows in the living room. Anne-

Marie had told her that it was the only present she had ever received from her husband. He had brought it to her when he had returned from the Far East after his first tour of duty in 1940. That would have been the first of many, Claire mused sadly, but her husband had been killed in action only six weeks later. They had been married only a year. Claire knew that even though Anne-Marie had never remarried, she'd led a reasonably happy life, treating Claire as the daughter she'd never had.

Well, it wouldn't be too long now before she reached the familiar cottage; then she would be safe....

A couple of hours later, Claire stopped the car in front of Anne-Marie's little house and honked the horn, feeling more serene than she had for days. A plump figure, enveloped in a gleaming white apron, appeared at the front door, shading her eyes against the late-afternoon sun. Then her hand flew to her mouth, and lifting her skirt hem with the other hand, she hurried toward the car, a joyous and incredulous smile lighting up her face.

"Claire ... my dear! Is it really you? How wonderful! I haven't had a letter from you this week, and I was just this minute wondering what you were up to. Come in!"

Quite unexpectedly, wrapped in her old nanny's comforting and loving embrace, Claire burst into tears. Still sobbing, she allowed herself to be led into the house.

"Poor thing, you're quite exhausted ... and so pale! The first thing you're going to do is go straight to bed. Your room is ready for you, as usual," Anne-Marie said, bustling upstairs with Claire's suitcase. "Now, just you lie down and sleep as long as you like. I'll be here when you wake up and then I can catch up on all your news." Tucking the comforter around her just as she did when Claire was a little girl, Anne-Marie kissed her and left the room.

Claire woke slowly. She was reluctant to open her eyes. Warm and rested, she could feel the comfort of the down-filled mattress beneath her body. She must have been sleeping for a long time, she thought, because the room was dark. Finally, she opened her eyes to see that the heavy curtains were blocking the light from outside. She was in her old room at nanny's, the one that looked out over the wood.

She heard someone moving around in the next room, and the door was pushed open very gently. Anne-Marie came in. Claire didn't want her to know she was awake just yet; she needed time to collect her thoughts and figure out what she was going to say. She wanted to tell Anne-Marie that life in Neuilly had been unbearable, but she was unanxious to broach the subject immediately, knowing that her nanny would be upset. She also realized, however, that all her nanny had to do was look in her eyes and she would read her mind like a book.

The woman leaned over the bed and put her hand on Claire's forehead.

Claire opened her eyes. "Oh, nanny . . . I missed you so much. . . ."

"Claire, my dear! I'm so glad you're awake. Are you feeling better now? You haven't been taking very good care of yourself, now, have you?"

She went to the window and opened the curtains.

Coming back to the side of the bed, she took hold of Claire's wrist.

"I think you're running a fever; I'll go next door and call the doctor."

"No, don't. I was cold on the way up, but I feel fine now. Please, nanny, I don't want a doctor," insisted Claire, seeing that Anne-Marie was ready to leave. "But I haven't had anything to eat for ages!"

"Good heavens! Why ever not?"

She scurried out of the room, but was back in ten minutes, carrying a tray of smoked ham, buttered biscuits, some cream cheese and a mug of hot, bubbling cider.

Claire devoured the food. Emotional upheaval had done nothing to diminish her appetite. Everything was delicious.

Anne-Marie silently took note of the young girl's pallor, the darkened circles under her large brown eyes, and the slight tremble of her hands, but made no comment as she sat on the edge of the bed.

"Let me look at you, my pet. It seems such a long time since I saw you last."

"Oh, nanny, you can't imagine how happy I am to be here with you!" Claire's eyes stung with emotion as she gazed at the kind face that showed so little evidence of the ravages of time. Her hair was pulled back into a bun and covered with a lace bonnet. Anne-Marie was not wearing the traditional dress of the region, but a light blue smock, which looked as though it had been washed and ironed that very minute. She kept the traditional dress—the long black skirt with velvet ribbons and an embroidered bodice— for festive days.

Claire had an urgent need to talk. She had come to the end of her resistence and could not keep her secret any longer.

"Nanny, would you mind very much if I stayed with you? I don't just mean for my vacation, this time . . . I mean permanently."

"My dear Claire, you know very well that this house is yours. Why do you ask such a question?"

To Claire it seemed that her nanny's gentle blue eyes were looking right through her. "Now tell me what's wrong," Anne-Marie said, her hands folded. "And don't leave out anything." Then she added more gently, "You know that there's nothing you can't tell me. What is it that's bothering you?"

"Nanny, how did my mother die?"

Anne-Marie was visibly taken off guard, and for a minute remained silent. Claire, sensing that her nanny was keeping something from her, became more determined than ever to learn the truth.

"Nanny!" she cried desperately. "Please, I've got to know the truth."

"The truth? But my dear girl, you already know it. Your mother died accidentally, on Christmas night."

"What kind of an accident was it?"

In her agitation, Claire failed to notice Anne-Marie's slight hesitation. "She was skating on a pond, and the ice gave way. She . . . drowned."

"Where did it happen?"

"In Brittany, on the grounds of your grandfather's château—"

"How many ponds are frozen over at Christmas-time in this part of the world?" interrupted Claire. She sat up straight in the bed. "Don't talk to me as if I were a child, please, nanny! My mother committed suicide, didn't she? She . . . she killed herself!"

"I would like to know who told you a farfetched story like that!" replied Anne-Marie heatedly. "You couldn't possibly have dreamed it up. No one was with your mother at the time, so it would be impossible for anyone to say what really happened."

"But, before that, wasn't she always . . . sad?"

"Well . . . ." Anne-Marie heaved a sigh. "Claire, why are you asking me all this now?" The old woman was carefully observing Claire's face as she began to talk, trying to see beyond her words and assess the degree of despair she was suffering. But the girl knew her nanny well, and somehow managed to keep the whole truth from her.

Claire described her life at Neuilly, with a stepmother who despised her and a father who appeared not to care very much about her one way or the other. She tried to be scrupulously fair in this description, knowing that her nanny would be able to tell instantly if she were exaggerating.

Then she related the conversation she had overheard while sitting in her old nursery, but felt too ashamed to mention the burden of heredity that she was carrying, or what the results would inevitably be. And while she did mention, however, how quick she was to anger on discovering the maid, Jeanne, in her room, Claire deliberately refrained from mentioning anything about her conversation with the count, hoping Anne-Marie would simply assume that Claire had left after breaking off with Oliver. All during her narrative Claire watched Anne-Marie's face closely for any reaction.

The room had become quite chilly by the time Claire had finished talking. Anne-Marie went to the fireplace and threw a handful of pinecones onto the dying embers. The flames shot up to brighten the room, and turning around, Anne-Marie saw that Claire had started to cry.

Touched, but holding back the soft words that sprang to her lips, she steeled herself to say the words she knew were necessary. "Now," she began, "I'm going to tell you exactly what I think, young lady. You have no business listening in on other people's conversations."

"But I wasn't trying to listen.... Not at first, anyway." Claire tried to brush away the tears, but not even the snowy white handkerchief that Anne-Marie handed her a second later would stem the flow.

"You could have closed the door instead of listening to that old gossip, Mrs. Martineau. You know very well what she's like: anything for a good story!"

"Just the same, you aren't denying the truth of what she said."

"Truth! Who knows what truth is? Meanwhile, I'll bet you think you're sick, but I've got news for you, missy: you're as healthy in mind and body as I am! The only thing wrong with you is that you were a very spoiled child, and you've always done exactly what you wanted to do. If only I could have stayed with you. Whims, temper tantrums! What you should have had was a good spanking together with a lot of love and cuddling. Still—" Anne-Marie smiled at Claire affectionately, "—you seemed to have turned out all right, my friend!"

Anne-Marie paused for a moment, then continued.

"Tell me, Claire, this man Oliver...do you regret having broken off with him?"

"Oliver was a very good friend, nothing more. I don't think I'll ever be able to love anyone...not really."

"Nonsense, that's your head speaking, not your heart. Love comes whenever and wherever it chooses, and usually when we least expect it. Now go back to sleep and forget all this. You can stay here as long as you like. You know I love to have you here. What you really need right now is some fresh air and a good long rest. Then you'll be as right as rain."

As Claire curled up again beneath the cozy eiderdown, she turned over Anne-Marie's words in her mind. Though she felt a little comforted, nothing her nanny had said diminished to any appreciable extent the horror of the conversation she'd overheard at the château.

When Claire finally slept, her dreams turned to nightmares.

Chapter 6

Several weeks went by. Claire and Anne-Marie celebrated Christmas quietly together, the happiness of the day only temporarily interrupted by Claire's adamant refusal to contact her father. In those weeks, the old woman showered her with love and attention, but was concerned that she had not been able to bring the color back to Claire's cheeks or the sparkle to her eyes.

Mrs. Martineau's words troubled Claire to the point of obsession. She began to watch herself very closely for signs of instability. She started to analyze her every thought, move and word, watching—almost hoping—to see some indication of madness. She had never loved anyone but her father and nanny, and interpreted this to mean that she must surely be suffering some kind of emotional deficiency. Even her good qualities became suspect. She had always tried to be straightforward and frank with everybody. Now she wondered if what she had thought to be a desire for honesty might really have been a secret wish to hurt people.

Little by little, she was creating a world of fantasy where only she could live. In a constant state of worry, she became increasingly subdued and withdrawn.

Anne-Marie took her to visit friends and neighbors in the hope that seeing other people would take her mind away from herself, but Claire remained pale and silent. Her only pleasure was walking in the countryside with Duke, the enormous part Collie that Anne-Marie had rescued from a pond three years earlier. Apparently the dog had been abandoned and had somehow fallen into the water. Anne-Marie had carried the shivering little puppy home in her arms and nursed it back to health. Now Duke was full grown and Anne-Marie's constant companion. When Claire arrived, she and Duke became fast friends and were soon inseparable.

One morning, Claire decided to save Anne-Marie a trip by going to get some kindling for the fire. She started off with Duke at her side as usual.

Having determined that morning to put aside her analytical introspection—at least temporarily—she made a conscious effort to enjoy the fresh air and verdant countryside, and to that end deliberately chose an unfamiliar path through the woods. Throwing a stick for Duke to retrieve, Claire's eye was suddenly caught by a glimpse of water through the bushes. She walked toward the clearing, recalling how, when she had been a child, she had imagined fairies and wood nymphs hiding behind every tree. She reached a spot where there were a great many dead branches and began to break them up so she could carry them back.

She couldn't remember having come upon this particular place during any of her previous walks. As she gathered up the dead wood a thought crossed her mind. Had her mother been out for a walk like this, on a similar kind of day? What was it that the old busybody, Mrs. Martineau, had said? Oh, yes... something about all the members of her family having an irresistible attraction to water. . . .

Claire wondered if the pond might have the same sort of fascination for her. Would she be drawn into it by some mysterious force? Was she afraid of death? She realized that the thought had never really occurred to her before.

Slowly, she approached the pond. Surprised that the dog was not at her side, she looked back. He was standing some distance behind, his tail between his legs, his head down, refusing to come any closer.

"Duke! Come on, boy! Come!"

Ordinarily, the words would have brought him galloping to her side, tail wagging. This time, they brought a slight whimper, as Duke slowly lowered himself to the ground, trembling.

"Well, all right... have it your way." Claire edged closer and closer to the water's edge; the bank was some three feet about the water. Bulrushes rose above the surface of the glittering pond. The water was opaque, making the depth of the pond impossible to determine.

Claire leaned forward and looked at her reflection in the water, but it quickly became distorted as a slight breeze rippled the water. She stretched herself out on the ground and bent her head until her golden hair touched the surface of the water.

It must be a wonderfully peaceful feeling, she mused, just to let oneself go... simply slide into this fluid universe. . . . She could forget all her troubles and give herself over to the cool caresses of the water.

She put one finger into the pond, then her whole hand. The cold startled her, and slimy weeds wound around her wrist. Fascinated, she couldn't take her eyes off the weeds that were wrapping themselves loosely around her arm, as if with a will of their own. She seemed hynotized.

She attempted to remove the weeds with her other hand, but succeeded only in causing both arms to become entangled. The weeds, sinister now, seemed determined to drag her into the water. Frantically, she began to struggle.

Slowly her body began to slide forward. In a flash, her mother's face appeared in her mind. Claire scrambled desperately, trying to find a grip on the smooth, muddy bank. She found none, and the murky water closed inexorably over her, with scarcely a ripple.

CLAIRE'S FIRST THOUGHT was that she had not expected death to be uncomfortable. She was lying on her back and beneath her was something hard and bumpy. Then, something warm and soft touched her face. As her senses came to life she tasted the putrid water in her mouth and felt sick.

She was conscious of physical pain, and at the same time realized that although she was very much alive, she was disoriented. She opened her eyes, but found herself looking into a bright noonday sun. She turned her head to one side and saw the large, soaking wet body of Duke lying beside her. He whimpered and wagged his tail.

Claire was stretched out across the pathway, and

stones were digging into her back. Easing herself
slowly into a sitting position, she wrapped her arms
around Duke's neck and hugged her faithful friend.
The dog pulled himself away, ran a little way up the
path, and came back to her, barking. He wanted to go
back to the house.

She tried to imagine what kind of strength he had
had to muster to get her out of the water. Somehow
overcoming the slimy fingers of the weeds, he had
dragged her across the pond to the other side, where
the edge was sloped, and pulled her from her liquid
grave.

They both ran back to the empty house, and Claire
hurried to change into dry clothes before Anne-Marie
returned. Trembling from the cold and filled with
dread, she was at least certain of one thing: Mrs.
Martineau had been right.

Duke stood in front of the fireplace and shook
himself. Then he stretched himself out on the warm
tiles in front of the fire and gave a throaty growl of
contentment.

Claire came out of her room as soon as she heard the
click of the garden gate. When Anne-Marie came into
the house, she saw Duke lying in front of the fire,
which was unusual for him; with his thick coat, he
normally chose a spot well away from the heat.

"Good morning, dear. Did you enjoy your walk?"

"I had a nice walk, yes.... And what have you
brought back, nanny?"

"Quail. Two beautiful birds that I'll cook with leeks
and butter. You must be starving."

She took the birds out of her basket. Duke lifted his
head, catching the scent of the poultry, then got up
and walked over to Anne-Marie. Absently, she

stooped to pat his head and then stopped, astonished. She stared at the dog's wet coat, then turned, white faced, to Claire. "Oh! Claire . . . Claire . . ." she murmured, her voice barely audible.

"What is it? Nanny, whatever's wrong?"

"The dog. . . ."

"What about him? He went for a swim, that's all."

"Claire, don't lie to me. You . . . you must have fallen into the water."

"But . . . ."

"Yes, you must have been in trouble for that dog to have jumped in after you."

"How do you know?"

"Because I've never been able to get Duke to put even a paw in the water ever since I rescued him from the pond. He's normally terrified of the water. Oh, Claire, you're so pale! Sit down, and I'll get you some hot broth."

Five minutes later, Claire felt the warm liquid spreading comfort through her body. She kept her eyes fixed on Anne-Marie. "I fell into the water, nanny. But not the way you think. I slid in . . . slowly . . . at first, deliberately. It was as if some strange force were pulling at me . . . some . . . ."

"You're talking nonsense, Claire," Anne-Marie interrupted sharply. "If you're trying to say that the water had some bizarre sort of effect on you, then certainly it's the first I've heard of it. Don't you remember the trips in the rowboat you and Francine used to take across that pond? The two of you used to imagine that you were going across the ocean to see the world! What's got into your head now?"

"Nanny, I really believe that some obscure force dictates our every move and that I'm no longer responsible for what I do or who I am.... It's hard to explain... I really had no premeditated suicide plan, but when I looked into the water I became mesmerized. Only when I really felt myself going under, did I make any effort to get out of the water."

Anne-Marie raised both her hands to her cheeks, but to hide the anguish she was feeling, spoke in a harsh voice. "I've never heard of anything so ridiculous in my life! And I always thought you were so sensible! What you need, my girl, is something to do! You're much too tied up in yourself. You're becoming altogether too withdrawn. If you were to give a little more thought to the future, instead of letting yourself get carried away with all these silly ideas, you—"

"But I can't seem to get interested in anything," protested Claire. "I don't even care if I go back to university! Anyway, what's the point?"

"Well, then, forget about going back to school! Find something else to do. Taking care of children...or sick people.... I don't know, Claire, there must be something!"

"If I could believe that a job could cure me, it would make everything very simple."

"Cure you! I explained to you before; there's absolutely nothing the matter with you. Mind you, if you keep telling yourself that you're sick, you soon will be. And if you go on thinking about nothing or no one except yourself, pretty soon your heart will dry up and wither like an old apple!"

In spite of her agitation, Claire couldn't help smiling at the old woman's analogy. She knew how much Anne-Marie loved her and just wished she could find it in herself to accept this fact—simply and appreciatively.

"But I *am* sick, nanny," replied Claire. "What's happening to me now is simply the result of—"

"You don't really know what you want," interrupted Anne-Marie. "You came here to start all over again and you think it's going to happen just like that. A person can't change, my dear, without making a little effort. You have to try to forget your unhappiness at the château, and your mother's death. Work at becoming interested in something, never mind about the past. Forget that you're Claire de Montebourg and get yourself a job!"

"Oh, nanny, if only I could," sighed Claire.

"And why not?" queried Anne-Marie briskly. "You're sitting here, fading away, not doing anything constructive. Why don't you go skiing for three or four weeks and then come back and look for a job? It would certainly make more sense than aimlessly running around in circles, like Duke chasing his tail!" She hesitated for a moment, then went on. "You'll need some money. I have a little I can give you, I don't spend very much here. I had thought about having running water put into the house, but I really think I might miss my well!" She opened the door of the kitchen cupboard and reached to the very back of the shelf. Her hand reappeared holding a cookie jar.

Claire was extremely touched. Since she had arrived, she had never asked herself whether Anne-Marie's resources would be enough to feed an extra mouth. Such matters never entered her mind. To Claire, having money was as natural as breathing or sleeping.

"Oh, nanny, thank you, but I have all the money I need, at least for a skiing holiday," Claire exclaimed, as she quickly figured out how much it would cost to replace the equipment she had left behind in Neuilly, and to rent a hotel room. "Please put your money away. I'll use the money my father gave me for Christmas. After that...." She hesitated. "After that's gone, I'll get a job."

The remainder of the afternoon and evening passed with Claire and Anne-Marie discussing a variety of subjects, with no further mention made of the incident in the pond or Claire's future employment. But after retiring to their rooms for the night, both fell into fitful, troubled sleeps.

Chapter 7

The train was slowing down as it neared the station at Sallanches, and passengers rushed to the windows for their first glimpse of snowy Mont Blanc, the highest and most beautiful mountain in the French Alps.

Tired after the long trip, which she had spent sitting in an uncomfortable carriage, Claire paid little attention to the glorious view that her fellow travelers were finding so exciting. She would rather have slept. A fretful, crying child in the compartment had kept her awake most of the night. She made a mental note to book a berth in a sleeping car for the return trip to Paris. She would have to economize some other way.

It was a new experience for Claire, having to travel like this. For the first time in her life she was conscious of money. A month at the hotel, ski equipment and train fare would all add up. She could not afford to travel first class, nor would she be staying at the kind of exclusive resort to which she was accustomed. She had made reservations at Croix-Haute, a relatively small and modest resort. The travel agent had assured her, however, that the rooms were comfortable and the food excellent.

The train pulled into the station, and Claire picked up her suitcase and followed the boisterous, jostling crowd of vacationers. She stood outside the station, and though the early-morning sun was bright, the mountain air was crisp and cold, and Claire found herself shivering.

She looked around the busy square for a bus that would take her to the village of Croix-Haute. There was no sign of one.

"Taxi, miss? Are you going to Megève?"

"No, Croix-Haute."

"I can take you there. There will be a bus, but not for another hour and it'll be very crowded. It's the only one of the day."

Claire didn't hesitate, even though she realized how much a taxi would cost. She was too eager to get to her room at the hotel and rest than to worry about how much the taxi was going to cost.

As the car made its way up the winding road, she looked out of the window idly . . . and caught her breath. On one side of the road, there was nothing but a sheer drop of some 1200 feet. The road had been chiseled out of the side of the mountain. Claire felt sick—was it just hunger and fatigue? She forced herself to look down at the gorge far below, and her feeling of nausea got worse. The emptiness of the gorge held a strange kind of attraction for her, and the scenery appeared to be shifting beneath her gaze. She closed her eyes against the sudden feeling of terror that seized her.

The sound of the driver's voice calmed her a little, and she opened her eyes. "We're almost there," he said, indicating with a nod of his head the village they were rapidly approaching. "Which hotel is it?"

"The Grand-Rocher."

A minute or two later, the taxi drew up in front of the hotel. Skis and toboggans leaning against the wall gave evidence of the activities being carried on by the guests, but at this time in the morning, most of them would still be sleeping. As Claire and the taxi driver walked up to the front door, the double doors opened and a tall man in a ski-patrol jacket and matching navy blue warm-up pants greeted them genially.

"Good morning! Come in!"

Claire walked into the lobby. She identified herself at the front desk, then a cheerful-looking young maid came and took her suitcase.

"Louise, take Miss Montebourg to number three and then show her into the dining room. She may want some breakfast. I hope you enjoy your stay here with us, *mademoiselle*," the man who greeted her said with a smile. "I'll introduce you to the other guests at lunchtime."

Murmuring her thanks, Claire followed the maid to her room. She was delighted to find it both clean and comfortable. The walls were a light shade of green and complemented the simple, dark wooden furniture.

"If there's anything you need, please just ask," Louise said hospitably. "You'll like this room, it faces east, so you'll get the morning sun."

Claire thanked the maid then walked over to the balcony. Having just come from the bleak Brittany coast, she found the spectacular scenery dazzling. The mountains were majestic and the snow sparkled brilliantly on the peaks. The white outlines were startlingly vivid against the blue sky.

"What's the name of that mountain . . . the one on the left with the three peaks?" Claire asked Louise who was still in the room.

"The Charvin. The long series of peaks on the right is the Aravis chain. If you go to the very top on the lift, you can see Mont Blanc and Chamonix. Now, if you would like some breakfast . . . ."

Claire ate heartily. The freshly baked biscuits were smothered in honey, and the coffee was hot and aromatic. Any doubts Claire may have had about the quality of the hotel food vanished.

After breakfast she went into the ski shop at the end of the long front hall of the hotel. It was really no more than a room with a mirror on one wall. But it had displayed a number of bright fashionable ski outfits as well as accessories such as goggles and wax, and Claire was able to buy all the clothing she needed right there. Having made her purchases, she decided to wander into the village of Croix-Haute for a little while. She passed children on their way to school, brightly decked out in patterned toques and matching mittens. Most of the stores, Claire noticed, sold ski outfits and equipment, but she saw several bakeries and a shop selling delicious imported chocolate from Switzerland.

By noon, Croix-Haute was filled with people. The skiers who'd gone out in the morning were heading back to their hotels and chalets. The village had come alive for another day.

Somewhat uneasily, Claire began to walk back to

the hotel. Never at ease meeting new people, Claire felt particularly self-conscious now that she was aware of her illness, and she wondered wretchedly if it had started yet to affect her actions. . . . Perhaps she should ask for a table by herself, and not go through the agony of trying to act and sound perfectly normal and happy. People would start to realize after a while; perhaps by her expression, or an action. . . .

Claire's thoughts were interrupted by the voice of Marcel Ravenaz—the owner of the hotel and the man that had met her at the door that morning—who said with a smile, "Miss Montebourg, I thought you would prefer to sit with some of the other guests rather than by yourself. If you're agreeable I'd like to introduce you to a charming young woman, who I think you'll like."

Nodding her agreement, Claire had to admire the man's diplomacy. He would have had a very difficult time finding her a free table. Claire did not argue with the man or demur, in spite of her indecision a few minutes earlier and followed him to a table by the large bay window, where a young girl about Claire's age sat reading a newspaper.

"Monique, may I introduce our new guest, Claire Montebourg."

The woman getting up from her chair to greet Claire was very tall. Extremely slim, she had a small face framed by a mass of blond hair. She had large blue eyes and a welcoming smile.

"Is this your first time at Croix-Haute?" she asked Claire when they were both seated.

"Yes, isn't it marvelous? I've never seen anything so picturesque."

"Picturesque and friendly, too," said Monique. "Have you been skiing, yet?"

"No, not yet. I was a little tired this morning after the train trip from Paris. I've come from Brittany and had to change trains in Paris. I'll probably go out after lunch, though."

A group of young people entered the dining room and came over to speak to Claire's companion.

"Hi, Monique! Are you coming with us this afternoon? Marcel is taking us over to the other side of the mountain."

"I'd like to, if the runs won't be too difficult."

"Don't worry about that," said a tall, redheaded man. "It's almost a beginner's trail over there, and Marcel has assured me the runs themselves are intermediate level only."

Monique turned to Claire. "Would you like to come with us? If you've done some skiing before, this will be perfect for your first time out this year. Marcel is a very good instructor, too," she added, seeing Claire's hesitation.

"He owns the hotel, doesn't he?"

"Yes. Here in Croix-Haute, the hotel owners are ski instructors in the winter and guides in the summer."

"Is this your first time here?" asked Claire.

"Oh, no! I've been coming here for four years, now. The same crowd seems to come year after year. Are you a student?"

"Yes . . . I'm studying law. And you?"

"I'm in my last year of Teacher's College in Lyon. Are you going to be staying here long?"

"I'm not sure . . . about three weeks—perhaps a month."

"Lucky you. I can only stay for a week. Most of the people here are students and you only see them on weekends. How can you get so much time off?"

Louise brought their lunch, and with the interruption, Monique's question was left unanswered, much to Claire's relief. The food was excellent, certainly as good as at any hotel in which Claire had ever stayed. She forgot all her reservations and began to enjoy her lunch with an enthusiasm that almost matched her companion's.

Suddenly the room became quiet, as everyone stopped talking. Claire looked up to see what was happening.

A young woman had entered the room, and the first thing Claire noticed was a profusion of ash-blond hair cascading in soft waves, down to the woman's shoulders. As she walked, her hips swayed beneath a tight, emerald green dress.

The newcomer turned around. She had the face of a model, with green eyes and beautifully molded cheekbones. She passed a table where some ten students were sitting, greeting them with an affected wave of her hand as she went by on her way to join an older couple at the back of the room.

There was a murmur of appreciative comments from the group of students.

"Her name is Christine and she's absolutely unbearable," said Monique in a whisper. "The silence we just witnessed is a must when she comes into a room. She likes to create a sensation wherever she goes. She was furious with her friends for ignoring her 'grand entrance' the other day and she always makes a point of arriving late so she can be noticed."

"Have you known her long?"

"She's been coming here for three years, so I see her, but I can't really say that I know her very well."

The volume of the conversation level returned to normal, and Claire and Monique returned their attention to their lunch.

Chapter 8

The next day Claire was sitting, reading, in the small sunny sitting room reserved for guests who wanted to stay in the hotel during the day but away from the noise in the larger games room.

It was almost time for lunch and the skiers were coming back from the slopes. Claire felt like being alone; she had taken a two-hour lesson with Marcel and was now very tired. She admired the expertise of her new friends and wanted to learn to ski as well as they did.

Bits and pieces of the conversations in the front hall reached her, distracting her from her book.

The door to the hallway opened and there was a sudden silence.

Christine making an entrance again, thought Claire. But then loud greetings were heard coming from all directions.

"What a lovely surprise!"

"Here's our champion skier!"

"How did you get here? Did you take the bus?"

Then Christine's affected drawl. "Finally, I can start to live again, and things around here won't be quite as boring!"

"Hi! Hello! Greetings, everyone! Philip, how are you! And Chris, beautiful as ever, I see!"

That voice.... Claire sat frozen. Where had she heard it before? Somewhere, out of the past, that deep voice with the touch of irony to it....

She moved her chair slightly so she could see into the hall; her face grew warm. Claire thought she must be dreaming. The new arrival was Dr. David Heron.

She started to get up to escape to her room, then changed her mind.

Perhaps he won't see me, she thought.

Claire smiled to herself. *Well, at least I'll be the exception!*

The bell rang for lunch. Hoping to escape everyone's notice, Claire headed straight for the dining room. Monique joined her a few minutes later. Having just got back to the hotel, she was not aware of the new guest's arrival.

A group of students came in, and with them David Heron. Seeing Monique, he greeted her cheerily.

"Hello, Monique! What's the snow like?"

"Dave! Great to see you!"

He turned and looked at Claire, and they found themselves staring at each other. Monique introduced them. "Dave Heron, Claire Montebourg."

Dave smiled, bowing slightly. "I'm very happy to meet you, Claire.

His eyes were mischievous. "You look remarkably like a friend of mine, Francine Severac. Would you have a relative of that name, by any chance?"

"No," answered Claire shortly, furious with herself for blushing.

"Claire's going out with our group. We hit the slopes at two," said Monique. "Are you coming with us, Dave?"

"Love to," he replied with a smile. "See you later."

With a wave of his hand he walked over to the owner, who had just come in.

"Welcome back, my dear doctor," said Marcel. "I see you've at last decided to take a vacation. Good! And I'm delighted that you've chosen to take it here! Now, where can I seat you? Some people will be leaving tonight, but until then, things are a little crowded." He hesitated. Then, with a small smile at Christine, he went over to Monique. "Monique and Claire, would you mind if the doctor joined you? This is the only table where there are only two people."

"My pleasure!" Monique answered, and as Dave was looking at Monique, he didn't notice the alarmed expression on Claire's face.

AFTER LUNCH, the group waited at the ski lift for Marcel. Christine arrived, dressed in scarlet ski pants and an ocelot jacket. Her hair was pulled back and partly covered by a red toque that matched her pants exactly. She looked around and frowned. "Isn't Dave coming with us?" she asked petulantly.

"He's already gone up," said Monique. "He said he'd see us on the slopes."

"Where are we going?"

"We're going over to the other side of the mountain and then stopping for a snack at the chalet—the one at the top, where the cable car on the other side stops."

"It's not too easy to reach," said the tall man with

red hair. "As a matter of fact, some of us will find it quite difficult," he added, with a look at Christine's skin-tight pants.

"I heard you," said Christine, "but I thrive on adversity, dear boy."

A minute or two later, Marcel arrived. "All set? Well, let's go. We'll meet at the top of the lift."

"Marcel, wait! I'm not ready . . . I can't get my straps done up!"

"I'm not surprised," answered Marcel, as he bent down to help her. "With pants that tight, you can't even bend your knees!" Everyone laughed as they headed toward the gondola.

Claire was thankful that the car she rode up in was very crowded. She knew that as long as she didn't look down to the valley thousands of feet below, she would not be frightened. Making sure she was standing in the middle of the car with no chance of being able to see out the window, she allowed her thoughts to wander, and very soon they turned to Dave Heron. At lunch he had been very discreet, both about having met her before, and about her illness, which she felt sure he suspected. Yet, from time to time, when their eyes met, she had felt herself tremble. He had been looking at her as a doctor looks at a patient. His gaze had been searching. . . .

Dave was already waiting at the top of the lift when the rest of them arrived. Christine, however, did not emerge from the cable car with the others. When she finally arrived, the group set out, but before very long she was once more lagging far behind.

"Hurry, Christine," shouted Marcel. "We want to get in as much skiing as we can. But be careful when you go down the hill. I suggest you take it in long traverses, because these hills are steep and the skiing is very fast today."

There seemed to be no perceptible increase in Christine's progress.

When they finally left the trail and began the descent, everyone followed the instructor's orders. One by one, they traversed down the hill, each gradually falling into a rhythm.

Finally the chalet came into view. Perched high above the valley, it looked like a doll's house. The slope began to get steeper, and the skiers were taking more care, with longer and longer turns.

Claire was feeling quite proud of herself. Even at the hardest spots, she was managing quite capably.

The group came to the final descent, which was quite long.

Claire saw the first skiers greeting Dave, who had already reached the terrace. Feeling very sure of herself, she increased her speed. She felt very relaxed and happy, intoxicated by the fresh, pure air, the sun on the snow, the speed of her descent. As she skied she tried to keep an eye on Dave but without losing sight of the hill in front of her.

Blinded by the sun, she wasn't able to make out what it was Dave held in his hands. Finally, she was able to see that it was a movie camera. Suddenly feeling very self-conscious, she lost control of her skis, fell sideways and began to slide down the hill.

"Well, my dear!" Christine called as she passed her and came to a stop at the steps of the chalet. "That's really quite a good act you've got there—it almost looked like an accident!"

Claire shoved a pole into the snow and hoisted herself back onto her feet. It was only with the greatest effort that she was able to keep herself from making an angry retort.

Dave put away his camera, laughing, as he shouted to Claire, "Thanks a million! That's the best thing I've shot yet!"

As soon as they had eaten, Marcel began to get everyone moving again. He was eager to start the final descent. "Come on, everyone, let's get going. The sun's starting to go down, and it's going to be really cold by the time we get back to the hotel."

The group slowly left the warmth of the chalet and went outside to put on their skis.

Marcel gave careful instructions. "We'll go back by the road. It'll take us all the way into Croix-Haute. Leave one at a time. Snowplow whenever you need to brake. At the sharp turn, keep to the right and take it very slowly. Don't try to ski side by side, the road isn't wide enough. Dave, would you mind waiting till last? We don't want to lose anyone along the way."

They quickly reached the road that led to the town. Christine had somehow managed to leave next to last, just ahead of Dave. For the first part of the descent, everything went well. Then the sharp turn that Marcel had warned them about loomed into view. The road was very narrow and on one side there was a sheer drop of several hundred feet.

Once again, the drop held a strange fascination for Claire, and suddenly she was gripped by the same terror as before. She couldn't go any farther. She stopped, and closing her eyes, she leaned against a snowbank, pressing herself against it, away from the steep drop on the other side of the road.

She heard Monique coming up behind her. To hide her panic, she leaned over her skis.

"Something wrong?"

"No, just a loose strap."

"Okay. See you later."

Now Christine was coming. She looked at Claire, eyebrows raised, but continued on her way.

Claire straightened. She had to hide her fear from Dave. Gathering her courage, she began to ski again, concentrating on the road to avoid looking at the emptiness so close to her side.

No . . . she couldn't do it! She'd never be able to make the turn. She was sure she'd go over the edge. Abruptly, she came to a stop once more, leaning against the rocks at the side of the road. She could hardly see. Her terror increased with every passing minute. She'd been skiing for years, but never before had she experienced this sensation.

I feel as if there's another part of me that's watching my every move, she thought, horrified. *And it's trying to destroy my will. I have to put an end to this, once and for all! I'm the only one who can do anything about this thing that's growing in me!*

She was holding her poles with such violence that her hands began to ache.

Dave came up behind her and stopped. "What's the matter?" he asked.

"Nothing," replied Claire trying to keep her voice calm. "Don't worry about me. It's . . . just my knee. I must have wrenched it earlier when I fell."

Dave crouched down and started feeling her knee. Eyes closed, Claire stood rigid like a statue.

Dave straightened and took her by the shoulders. "Open your eyes and look at me. Are you really hurt?"

She tried to compose herself. She realized now that she could take off her skis and walk around the curve, keeping to the right side quite easily. She bent down to release her bindings.

Dave put out a hand to stop her. "You'll have a hard time walking on this slippery road. You'd be better off going very slowly on your skis."

His eyes seemed to be looking right through her. "This is the third time," he said softly. "The third time that I've caught you lying. Why, Claire?"

"What makes you think I'm lying?" Claire's voice trembled.

"I don't think anything's wrong with your knee. Why don't you admit that it's the turn that's bothering you? It bothers quite a lot of people. . . . That's the problem, isn't it?"

"Leave me alone," Claire snapped, feeling her composure crumble. She must not let Dave see how upset she was: her dizziness would simply be one more indication to him of her sickness. *He knows*, she thought; *he knows!*

"Orders are orders," commented Dave easily, not affected in the least by Claire's outburst. "I'm supposed to be rearguard, if you remember. What would Marcel say if I didn't bring you back safe and sound? At the moment, I'm sharing his responsibilities. And if you wait much longer before deciding to tell me the truth, we're going to have the whole rescue team coming back for you."

"I have nothing to tell you."

Dave stared at her intently, as if expecting her to change her mind and give him an explanation of her behavior. What seemed to Claire like hours later he finally said, as if reaching a decision, "All right. Then start skiing. Concentrate on the tips of your skis and don't look at anything else."

He positioned himself so that his skis were parallel to hers and he was between her and the emptiness on the left. Then he took her firmly by the arm.

Together they managed the dangerous curve in the road. From there on the road widened, cutting through a wood. Dave, still holding onto Claire, pulled her to a stop.

She looked at him gratefully, relief that the ordeal was over lighting her face with a smile. "Thank you, doctor."

Suddenly Claire thought about Christine and wondered if Dave considered the incident a few minutes earlier to have been engineered by Claire to get his attention. She was mortified that such a thought might occur to him and she leaned forward to push off ahead of him.

Claire's skis wouldn't move. Dave had crossed the back of them with one of his own, effectively preventing her from moving.

"Just a minute, Claire. You and I have a lot to talk about. I think, however, that we'll leave our conversation till another time. Have you ever seen the sunrise on Charvin?"

"No. . . ."

"Then I'm inviting you to see it with me. It's one of the most beautiful sights in this part of France. Tomorrow, seven o'clock, in the front hall. Agreed?"

"Agreed," said Claire, almost in spite of herself.

"Now, we'd better get going."

Christine saw them first. They were coming down, side by side. When they came to a stop close to the group, Christine had a biting remark ready for Claire.

"You're making Dave play a very dangerous game, my dear. He was skiing on the left side of the road.

There could have been a very serious accident, if a car had come up the road!"

"I think he's a good enough skier to be able to take care of himself," Claire responded mildly.

"What happened?" asked Marcel. "I was just getting ready to come back for you."

"Nothing serious," said Dave. "Just a little trouble with a strap."

Christine was the only one who took the trouble to look closely at the straps. There didn't appear to be anything unusual about them. She said nothing, but when she looked at Claire there was fire in her eyes

CLAIRE HAD TROUBLE GETTING TO SLEEP that night. Why had she agreed to meet Dave? What was she going to tell him? He always seemed to know that she was evading the truth. . . .

She remembered him again, skiing to the left of her, without concern for his own safety. He had protected her and helped her make that difficult turn. She should be grateful to him, but the thought of her own weakness humiliated her.

How could she hope to explain her feelings of dreadful anxiety? What could she do to keep the doctor from really finding out her secret? Could he see something in her face, a look about her eyes, that could be interpreted as a sign of madness?

She wouldn't go to meet him. It was the only solution. She would find some excuse. . . .

Having made that decision, she felt a little calmer and in a few minutes was fast asleep.

Chapter 9

At six-thirty the next morning, Claire leaped out of bed and ran to the window It was still dark outside, and the few remaining stars, sparkled through the clear air. It was going to be a perfect day.

Suddenly reversing her decision of the previous night, Claire started to get ready to meet Dave, humming a little tune under her breath.

Dave joined her as she came into the front hall. "Let's take our skis with us," he suggested. "We can leave them at the lift on our way by and save ourselves the trouble of getting them later. Now, about that knee . . . completely cured?"

"Oh, don't!" said Claire in a small voice. "You know as well as I do that there was nothing wrong with it." Dave smiled at her, saying nothing, and held the front door open for her.

They crossed the slumbering town and started up the winding road beyond it. Claire felt very shy in Dave's presence and waited for him to open the conversation.

He took her arm and turned her around. "Look!"

The whole range of mountains was slowly taking on a soft pink glow. The peaks of Mont Charvin stood out against a sky of palest blue. Down low in the valley, the last vestiges of twilight were disappearing. Then the direct sunlight hit the snow-covered fields and a million sparkles illuminated the glorious morning.

Claire was silent as she gazed at the awesome sight No words existed that would have been enough to express this beauty.

Dave said quietly, "You're the only woman I've ever known who hasn't talked nonstop about her admiration for a scene like this. I'm glad. Such beauty should be shared in silence."

Claire stepped away from him, releasing her arm from his light grasp before speaking "Is this a habit of yours, to bring women up here so they can pass some sort of a test? Are you classifying your psychological findings, as well?"

Dave burst out laughing. "Shall I tell you about my psychological findings this time? Well, I find that I'm dealing with a very enigmatic character. Too bad," he added, looking admiringly at Claire. "This light really suits you—or is that anger bringing such a blush to your cheeks?"

He moved closer to her. "Has anyone ever told you that you've got a little golden spot on the iris of your left eye?"

Claire turned away and abruptly started to walk along the road. Dave hurried to catch up with her "Not only was it extremely rude of you to walk away, but you didn't even wait until I'd completed my diagnosis. That spot in your eye says that you should be careful of your liver. What did you think I was going to say . . . tell you it was a symptom of insanity or something?" He laughed.

"I don't find that very . . . funny, Dave," Claire stammered.

Dave's eyes sparkled with mischief. Claire saw it and said that he never took anything seriously.

"Of course I do," he answered, "but with you, it's very difficult. Your back goes up at practically every word I say. . . . Let's keep going until we're up a little farther, shall we? The sun will warm us up."

After they had walked for a little while, Claire turned to Dave. "Why did you say that I'd lied to you three times, yesterday?"

"Well, there was yesterday for instance, with your knee. I'd like to know exactly what happened there."

"Are you asking as a doctor?"

"No, as a friend. Forget about my being a doctor. I was intrigued, that's all. Was it the drop at the side of the road that frightened you?"

"Yes. I . . . I was afraid I wouldn't be able to brake enough to make the turn."

The intent look he was giving her began to make her feel uneasy.

"Why didn't you just use the snowplow technique?"

"I don't know . . . maybe. . . . Oh, let's just forget about it. I'm beginning to feel ridiculous. Now, tell me, what's lie number two?"

"You seem to have forgotten, Miss Claire-Francine. I'd like to know why you didn't give me your real name, that night. What were you . . . what are you afraid of?"

"Nothing," she answered hotly. "I guess I was in a state of shock from the accident and didn't know what I was saying."

"The car belongs to you, doesn't it?"

"Yes, but . . . I didn't know who you were and I had a very good reason for not wanting anyone to know where I was headed."

Dave stepped back, still gazing at her intently. "Your life seems to be somewhat complicated, not to say mysterious," he said. "Nine o'clock at night in miserable weather, a young girl with suitcases in her car on her way to a secret destination . . . ."

Once again, Claire felt herself flushing. "And you've drawn your own conclusions, right?" she asked finally, a little note of bitterness in her voice.

Dave looked at her for some time without answering.

"Oh . . . you . . . you . . . ." Claire stammered and tears welled up in her eyes. "And you must all have thought me so rude for leaving without saying good-bye the next morning. Did your Aunt Suzanne get my thank-you note? I left it propped up on the dresser for her. But I *had* to keep moving—I had my reasons. You think I'm a compulsive liar just because I didn't give you the right answers that night. It's too difficult to explain it all, right now, but you've got to believe me!"

"Why were so frightened? Was someone following you?"

Claire looked down at the ground. "No . . . well, not exactly. . . ."

She looked up again and their eyes met.

"If you have any feelings for me at all, please don't ask me any more."

Dave took her arm. "Take it easy, Claire. I believe you, and I hope that you and I are going to be friends. Do you realize that I don't know a thing about you, except your name . . . and I'm not too sure about that!" he added, smiling.

"What's the third lie?" Claire asked curiously. "I've been trying to think what it could be. I really don't know that I told you another one. . . ."

"Well, perhaps it doesn't qualify, it's so small. A lie of omission, so to speak. Why did you register under the name of Montebourg?"

Claire threw back her head defiantly. "I didn't think it was necessary to include the 'de' at a small resort like this."

"You thought this simple hotel beneath your standards, unworthy of your rank, didn't you? Do you honestly think people care about the 'de' in your last name? If you don't act like a snob, Claire, you won't be treated like one."

"Why do you see something unpleasant in everything I say and do? If someone else had done it, you would have seen it as a simple decision not be pretentious."

"Maybe, but not in your case. You have a lot of pride, *Miss de Montebourg*. What do you do? Are you a student?"

"Yes. I'm studying law."

"Do you really want to become a lawyer, or are you just filling in time?"

"I've never actually asked myself that question," she answered slowly. "But I don't think I want to be a lawyer."

"Too bad. I think you'd be a good one," Dave said cheerfully. "But I would have thought you'd spend your time playing tennis, or riding, playing bridge, taking a few classes at the Sorbonne, going to elegant dinner parties, opening nights at fashionable theatres. . . . Am I right?''

The accuracy of Dave's remark made Claire self-conscious.

"What's so special about that? Any number of people are in precisely the same situation. Are you criticizing all of us?'' she asked defensively.

"Any number? I think you're exaggerating. I'd say that such young women are a rare species in this day and age. Take a look at our little group, right here. Monique is in her final year at Teacher's College. The two women at the next table are in their last year studying to be pharmacists. Philip is in engineering. They're all real students, not dilettantes. And they're studying in the most practical sense. When they graduate, they expect to work.''

"You're forgetting Christine,'' Claire said briskly. "She's probably never given a thought in her life to doing anything useful.''

"You're wrong there. She's a drama student and will likely be a very good actress. But let's drop the subject. Now is what's important; let's just enjoy it. See how beautiful the village looks from up here? Watch the sun as it starts to light up the rooftops. I love this place. Whenever I come here, all my worries seem to evaporate, and I get a tremendous feeling of peace.''

They continued their walk, slowly and in silence. When they got back to the ski lift, their skis were still the only ones there.

As they were putting on their skis, they noticed Monique and Philip, skiing quickly toward them.

"Hello," Philip shouted. "We've been looking everywhere for you!"

"Can you come to the hotel, right away?" asked Monique, panting. "Chris is very sick and her grandparents would like you to have a look at her."

"Didn't they call the local doctor?" asked Dave.

"Chris doesn't want any other doctor."

"All right, I'm coming. What's the matter with her?"

"Some kind of fever, I think," replied Monique. "Her grandmother says that she's been sort of delirious since really early this morning. When Christine didn't appear at breakfast, her grandmother went to find her."

Dave skied quickly toward the hotel.

Claire didn't believe for a minute that Christine was really sick. It was just one more pretext to have Dave at her side. She could imagine Chris lying in her bed, her hair carefully arranged on the pillow, eyes half-closed, trying every trick in the book to seduce Dave. The very thought of it made Claire angry, somehow.

"Come on, Claire," invited Monique. "Let's take a run or two before the class starts."

"There isn't much point in waiting for Dave," said Philip candidly. "Our future Sarah Bernhardt will be playing her big scene for hours!"

Claire followed them. The thought of Dave bending over Christine, lying in bed, plagued her and she found herself nonplussed by how much she was affected.

I'm being stupid, she reprimanded herself, firmly. *He's a nice man, but that's all.* She had enjoyed their early-morning walk, but, as she thought about it, she became aware that she was beginning to feel something a little beyond friendship for him. . . .

THAT EVENING AFTER DINNER, Philip announced the schedule of activities for the evening. "At nine-thirty, there's going to be a torchlight ski parade by the instructors. At ten, there'll be music and dancing at the disco and then—"

He was interrupted by a great shout of approval.

Claire didn't feel much like going out and wasn't particularly interested in dancing. She had seen Dave only briefly during dinner. Having called a colleague from Megève to see what should be done about Christine, he had had to wait for him inside the hotel almost all day.

When Christine, pale and drowsy, came down for dinner, Claire was quick to note the triumphant expression in her eyes. Christine refused to talk about her illness during dinner, and when Monique asked Dave about her condition, he had simply replied that she was better but he couldn't give out any details.

After dinner, Claire decided to get dressed and go out to watch the parade. If the instructors were going to the trouble of putting on the show, the least she could do was join in with the rest in showing her appreciation. She joined the others as they set out for the hill where the torchlight parade was taking place

Neither Christine nor Dave made an appearance.

In the distance, the fir trees blended with the night sky, and not even the bright whiteness of the ski hills pierced the darkness. Halfway down the slope was the chalet that was the focus of everyone's attention.

Soon, tiny pinpricks of light appeared by the chalet, and formed a whirling trail of fairy lights down the slope. As they approached the discotheque at the bottom, the lights grew larger, to become torches held aloft by the ski instructors, some of whom then proceeded to perform acrobatic feats, still holding their torches. The crowd hooted and yelled for a long time. Encouraged by the reception, the skiers decided to repeat their performance.

As the crowd was waiting, Claire heard a familiar voice behind her. "It's a bit silly to be out this late at night with only a light jacket on."

She turned to see Dave standing close behind her, smiling down at her. He put his arm around her shoulders, as though to share his own warmth with her. Instantly, Claire's unsociable mood disappeared. She wanted to shout and laugh with the others, but something held her back. She just couldn't seem to let herself go and show the joy she was feeling.

"Well, good evening," she said calmly, returning his smile "Your patient finally let you go, I see."

Dave ignored her remark. "Look," he said, pointing to the chalet, "they're starting again. That's Marcel, out in front. They're terrific, aren't they? I've been coming here for ten years, and they do it every single year, without fail. Let's go inside and propose a toast to them."

In no time the disco was crowded. Music filled the air and couples started to dance with great enthusiasm.

But the full day's skiing began to take its toll, and after only a couple of hours, the disco was all but empty, as weary couples wended their way back to the hotel.

Claire walked silently beside Dave. They had danced together several times and during the last slow dance, he had held her close to him. Even though it frightened her a little, she felt powerless to resist the strong feeling that had come over her.

She remembered something that Philip had mentioned, and decided to see if she could confirm it. "Is it true you'll be leaving in three days, Dave?"

"Unfortunately, yes. I was only able to get a locum—a replacement—for a week, so I have to go back. But . . . ." He hesitated for a moment before going on quietly. "Does that upset you?"

She didn't answer, and Dave continued. "My best friend will be arriving tomorrow, Peter Breveley. You met him at Aunt Suzanne's, remember? Would you like to spend Sunday with us? I mean the whole day. . . . I know that Peter wants to go to Chamonix. We can take our skis with us, and we'll bring you back here in the evening, on our way home. How does that sound?"

Without a moment's hesitation, she accepted.

Chapter 10

On Sunday, as Claire sat in the car listening to the two men talking, she experienced a feeling of warmth and contentment.

As she looked across at Dave, she wondered if he felt anything greater than friendship toward her. Certainly, friendship was very much to be valued, but she felt certain that some deeper emotion had developed between them at the disco, bringing them closer together.

Dave drove very carefully up the steep hill. When they reached the first plateau, Peter took the wheel. Then, after another few miles, they switched again. From time to time, Dave would turn his head to speak to Peter, and Claire would look intently at his classic profile. Several times, she caught the sparkle of his dark eyes as he turned to her, obviously aware of her scrutiny.

Would she have felt the same sensation if any other man had looked at her that way?

She imagined herself dancing with Peter. His

physique was similar to Dave's, and she liked his fine face and dark gray eyes, as well as the blond curly hair. Furthermore, he had never been sarcastic to her, as Dave had often been. Yet the thought of being in Peter's arms left her utterly indifferent.

What was it about Dave that was so special? She should really have declined the invitation to come along on this drive, Claire thought to herself. She should have left Dave at the discotheque with a smile and a firm handshake, thereby reaffirming her independence. She couldn't afford to become emotionally attached to Dave . . . or anyone. If Mrs. Martineau had been right, then her mind would begin to deteriorate It was a nightmare she would have to face alone Suddenly, Claire began to feel lonely, the ache of her separation from her father, and the knowledge that she had no future banished from her mind the contentment she had just been experiencing. She clenched her fists into tight balls and tried to turn her thoughts to something else.

Monique and the others were due back at school, and had left the night before, though Christine would be staying on for another few weeks. But there had been nothing sad in their farewells; they had promised to come back on weekends, as long as the good weather held. Ski weekends provided a welcome escape from their studies.

Claire smiled faintly as she imagined the look on Christine's face when she discovered the empty places in the dining room, and the subsequent lack of reaction as she walked in.

Peter's voice brought her out of her daydreaming. "Penny for them, Claire! You're smiling like the cat that ate the canary. I hope you were thinking of me!

I've asked you the same question three times now, without getting a reply. Would you rather have lunch in Chamonix, or at the chalet restaurant at Mont Brevent?''

"Either would be fine. It doesn't matter at all to me."

"Then we'll go to Mont Brevent, so we can go up on the cable car. Those open chair lifts at Chamonix are freezing!"

In a way, Claire was relieved, although she kept it to herself. The very thought of crossing a valley thousands of feet below in an open chair lift had been a source of terror to her ever since they'd started out.

The memory of that narrow road, with its sharp turn, still sent shivers through her body. The one thing she didn't want to do was to show these two doctors how neurotic she really was. She was determined not to give Dave any further reason to suspect her instability. He must leave thinking of her as a stable, well-adjusted woman.

THEY FINALLY ARRIVED AT Mont Brevent. The jagged peaks of Mont Blanc presented a breathtaking spectacle of white splendor. It was Nature at her very best.

They parked the car and walked with their skis to the gondola. Peter, who had promised to see two patients whom his father had sent to the hospital there, suggested that he meet them at the restaurant at the top where the lift stopped.

Claire and Dave arrived at the bottom of the lift just in time to board a cable car. It was swaying gently, as there were only a few people on board. Claire looked at the small cables with apprehension, but once the car began to move, her fears disappeared.

All the way up, Dave looked out the window of the

funicular, commenting on the beauty around them. Claire kept her eyes squeezed shut to stop her dizziness but listened as Dave described the extraordinary majesty of the mountains sparkling in the sunlight against the incredibly blue sky.

"Are we at 7500 feet yet?" she asked him.

"Not yet. We have to change to another cable car. Once we're there, we'll have a complete view of the whole range of mountains."

Claire felt herself stiffen with tension. She wondered if she'd be able to ward off the dizziness a second time. . . .

They boarded an empty car and Claire put her back to one window and stared at the floor. Slowly, the car started to glide along its cable, jerking slightly.

Looking up once, quickly, Claire realized that the valley had disappeared. They had ascended about halfway and by now the mountain was extremely steep. From one window she could only see an endless white mountain face. The car was thousands of feet above the floor of the valley.

In a world without dimension, Claire felt herself being pulled into a dark, bottomless pit. Perspiration broke out on her forehead. She didn't even realize that Dave had jumped up, and was holding her in his arms.

"Claire, try to relax. Hang on for another minute, we're almost there."

He was holding her tight, her face against his chest, hiding from her the enormous distance to the valley below. When they reached the platform at the top, she got out of the car and automatically took her skis out of the rack attached to the side of the cable car Dave's strong arm no longer supported her, but now, on solid ground, her dizziness vanished. They walked toward the sun-drenched terrace of Mont Brevent.

Gently Dave led Claire toward a corner table inside the chalet. They sat down and he put his arm around her shoulders, his hand cupping her upper arm. The tender, protective gesture troubled her, and when she turned to look at him, her eyes were once more filled with panic.

"Oh, Dave! This is so horrible!"

"I want you to tell me everything, Claire, from the very beginning. But this time, it's the doctor asking the questions. How long have you felt like this?"

"I don't really know . . . I can't tell you. . . ."

"Claire, please try to remember. Have you ever been in a serious accident? Ever had a blow on your head?"

"No."

"Then perhaps you have been through some kind of traumatic experience that has left its mark? It's the only explanation. Try to think. . . ."

"A terrifying experience? Yes, I guess you could call it that," said Claire, thinking back to the conversation she had overheard in her old nursery. "But I don't think it's that."

She turned to look at Dave. "Oh, Dave, can't you understand that you're only torturing me with these questions? We're going to be saying goodbye to each other tonight. Forget this. You've been telling me to live for the moment, enjoy what's happening right now. Don't let's ruin this moment. Let's just say I've got vertigo, and leave it at that."

"Claire, if you really are ill . . . I want to help. But I can't do anything, unless you're willing to help yourself."

"All right, then, I'll tell you everything. But you're not going to like it," she said, her voice hard. "Don't look at me, it only makes it more difficult. You think it's something quite simple, some little neurosis that can be cured easily. Well, it's much more serious than that. Sooner or later ... I'm going to go completely insane. I've felt the beginnings of it already. This dizzy feeling I get, whenever there's empty space around me ... and, worse than that, my obsessive attraction to water. Only a little while ago, I nearly drowned ... and I hadn't fallen into the water accidentally. I'd let myself slip in, gradually. I know that some day, I *will* drown, and not because I want to. That's the way my mother, and other of my relatives, died."

Tears blinded her, and she dropped her head into her hands, sobbing wretchedly.

Dave put his arms around her and spoke in a gentle voice. "Claire, I want you to listen carefully, and believe every word I'm going to say. I said before that I could help you, and it's true. But I can't do a thing without your cooperation. Was it the night of the accident, when I met you on the road, that you'd learned about your family?"

"The day before."

"I can appreciate what a horrible shock that must have been. But I still maintain you're not sick. But you seem to be introverted by nature, and now you've got the idea that you're going to commit suicide. Your being so withdrawn has destroyed your courage, and now you're seeking refuge in an imaginary illness. Is your father still alive?"

"Yes, but I've left home."

"Then how are you managing to live?"

Not in the least upset by the direct question, Claire replied just as directly. "I don't have any means of support. My father gave me quite a lot of money for my Christmas vacation and I've been living on that. I've never given much thought to the future . and now, even less."

"Have you thought about getting a job?"

"Yes, I've thought about it. But what kind of work could I do? I'm not qualified for anything! Besides, you seem to have forgotten, Dave—you can't fight that kind of heredity, no matter what you do!"

"There are very few mental disorders that can be inherited, Claire, despite what amateur psychologists have been saying for years. If there have been suicides in your family, it doesn't necessarily prove a thing. Each one of their motives might have been very different. Look, modern science has techniques that can detect even the slightest brain damage. When you get back to Paris, why don't you take some tests?"

"And if there is brain damage?"

"Then it can be treated. Medical technology today can perform miracles, Claire. But I have the feeling that you'll find that there's nothing organically wrong, and that your treatment will be mostly up to you. Get rid of the notion that you're sick and convince yourself that you're well, and don't let yourself dwell on things you find depressing or frightening." He pulled her closer to him. "Will you do it? Will you agree to get some tests done?"

Claire looked into his eyes and saw the sincerity there. A wave of tenderness washed over her. She wanted to rest her head against his shoulder and stay with him forever and she was entirely willing to follow his advice. "Yes, I'll do that. But first I'll have to find some kind of work to do. I couldn't bear to return to university, I never was very interested in law. And since I've left home, I have nothing to go back to, in Paris. Where can I get a job?"

"Don't you have any friends, or other family members that you could stay with?"

"Just one. I have an old nanny in Brittany. That's where I was headed when I got the flat tire."

"Listen, why don't you finish out your holiday here—it'll do you good—then go back to Brittany. Check the paper every day and try to find a job. I'll be thinking about you and also be on the lookout. I'll give you my address, and if you have any problems, I want you to promise to get in touch with me."

He looked at her intently, then asked, "How long do you expect to be staying here?"

Claire hesitated. "Another couple of weeks, provided my money holds out."

"I'll try to get away for another weekend and come and join you, but I can't promise anything. It'll depend on my patients. . . ."

Peter's cheery voice interrupted him. "I've been looking all over the place for you two!"

Claire pulled herself together as she left the warmth of Dave's arms. "Let's eat on the terrace," she suggested.

"Good idea," Dave agreed. "It's warmed up, now. Peter, come with me and we'll see if they can serve us out there."

"I'll stay and watch the skis," said Claire.

As she watched their retreating backs, she couldn't believe that Dave would be leaving that night, leaving her alone again.

Chapter 11

The following week, the ski resort was relatively quiet. Christine's appearances in the doorway of the dining room went almost unnoticed. Claire saw some new faces, but was not able to regain the contentment of the previous week.

After Dave left, she seemed to lose some of her determination. The thought kept slipping into her mind, unbidden, that in spite of any effort she might make, she would not be able to fight the nausea brought on by heights and the almost catatonic state that usually resulted. Dave was wrong: it hadn't been Mrs. Martineau's revelations that had provoked her illness. She had been sick long before she received that shock.

In fact, the first time she'd felt this terror was when she took her flying lessons with Oliver, a former bush pilot who had wanted to share with her the intoxication of wide open skies. She had learned to fly, thanks to him, but one day, at 9000 feet, she'd suddenly become dizzy and terrified of the height. Since that day, she had never flown again.

At times, she would react like that without apparent reason. From what depths of her subconscious did such forces come? Claire doubted all of Dave's medical science could do anything to help her. She had agreed to the tests, but did not hold out much hope.

Dave . . . would she ever see him again? He had spoken of a weekend, and Claire wondered if she would be able to afford to stay on long enough to wait for him.

Checking the money she had left, she counted it carefully and started to do some calculating.

She went over the figures several times and her heart sank. If she didn't spend another cent on anything else but food and lodgings, she would have just enough left to stay for another ten days. To be on the safe side, she really should leave within a week. She decided, however, that she would stay until her funds were completely used up; she would give up her skiing lessons and find out if there were trails available for cross-country skiing. That would be much cheaper as she wouldn't have to buy a lift ticket for the whole day.

Realizing her sorry financial position, Claire determined that as soon as her holiday was over, she would find a job, no matter what.

ONE DAY, WHILE RETURNING to the hotel, she had had an unpleasant meeting with Christine, who informed her casually, but with a self-satisfied smirk, that Dave had asked her to marry him, and that she had accepted. Claire felt as though someone had hit her. Dave had never given the slightest indication. . . .

When she got back to the hotel, the maid told her

that there was a letter for her. Upset by Christine's news, Claire became apprehensive about the letter. Was there something wrong with nanny...or with her father? Claire felt herself begin to tremble.

She walked quickly from the hall to her room and picked up the letter from the table. She recognized Anne-Marie's writing immediately. Fearfully, Claire opened the envelope and began to read. As relief spread through her body, her knees began to tremble in reaction and she walked over to the bed to sit down. As her tension dissipated, she burst into tears. She was so very happy to have news of the beloved old woman, and to find out everything was all right with her.

Christine spent all her afternoons in Megève. She and Claire, by implicit agreement, went in opposite directions.

On her own, Claire took leisurely walks in the neighboring countryside and took up cross-country skiing, which she thoroughly enjoyed. The trails were empty during the weekdays, as most of the vacationers preferred downhill skiing. She found the silence of the woods very soothing, and loved the dappled designs on the snow the sun created as it shone through the trees.

For two days, a warm wind had been blowing from the valley, giving rise to unseasonably mild weather. The weight of the winter clothing became uncomfortable, and more and more of the skiers were wearing jeans and light pullovers, without hats or jackets.

One day, Claire stayed in the hotel, and Marcel noticed her sunning herself on the balcony of her room. He greeted her warmly.

"Hello, there! Isn't it a marvelous day? It's like spring in the middle of February. Let's just hope the snow doesn't all melt! We're having a dance here tomorrow night, did you know?"

"Who's coming?" asked Claire, casually.

"Monique, Philip, some students from Lyon and a busload from Belgium. We're going to be filled to the rafters!"

Claire tried not to think about Dave. He'd said he'd come if he could, but it depended on the patients. . . .

"Be careful you don't get too much sun, Claire. It can be dangerous to lie in the sun too long at this time of year."

"No, Marcel, I won't. In fact, I was just thinking about going for a short ski."

"Oh! In that case, could I possibly ask a favor of you?" he asked.

"Of course, what is it?"

"Would you mind going past the garage and seeing if I left the key for locker three there? I seem to have misplaced it."

"Sure. I'll go and check it out, right now. I'll be back in about half an hour."

"Thanks very much."

Pleased to have something definite to do, Claire strapped on her skis and went down to the garage at the bottom of the hill. She found the locker open and the key in the lock, but when she tried to pull the key out, she found it was stuck. Her skis were making things a little awkward, so she kicked them off and jiggled the key to try to loosen it. Intent on what she was doing, she didn't notice that a car had pulled up behind her.

"What a lovely reception committee! How did you

know I was coming?" The familiar voice made her heart pound.

She turned around quickly. "Dave! It's you!"

"None other! I'm so glad to see you looking so happy—is it because I'm here? I'm really very flattered. Look at you, you're actually blushing! What have you been doing with yourself while I've been away?"

"Just relaxing. And yes, I'm glad to see you!" Claire said, picking up her skis.

"Just let me park the car and we'll walk up together," said Dave, getting back into the car.

As Claire turned toward the car, a motion in the passenger seat of Dave's car caught her eye.

Looking at Claire, a cool smile on her lips, sat Christine.

How did she know Dave was coming, Claire asked herself. Perhaps they really are engaged, after all.

Turning away quickly, she lifted her skis to her shoulder and walked briskly back toward the hotel without a backward glance.

Back in her room, Claire threw herself down on the bed, the ache in her heart a physical pain. So this is what she'd been waiting for so anxiously! How ridiculous she'd been to even imagine that he was coming back to see her!

There was a light knock on the door and Louise, the maid, came in. Claire sat up abruptly, smoothing her hair nervously back from her flushed face.

"Excuse me, miss, I didn't know you were here. I was just coming in to close the shutters and turn down the bed."

She noticed that Claire was now very pale. "Are you feeling all right?" she asked solicitously.

"I'm fine, thanks Louise. Just a little too long in the sun, that's all. I have a small headache, it'll go shortly."

"Dr. Heron just arrived, would you like me to call him for you?" asked Louise innocently.

"No, thank you! I think I'll go for a walk. Fresh air will clear my head, I'm sure."

Outside, Claire bumped into Dave walking up the road.

"What happened to you? I just went to park the car, and when I came back, you were gone."

"I had the distinct impression I was . . . an unwelcome third, that's all." Claire bit her lip to stop it from trembling.

David looked at her quizzically, a frown on his face. "And what, may I ask, gave you that impression?"

"You know the answer to that one much better than I do!" Claire retorted. "Why should I stay? You're here to see Christine, so why don't you just go and see her, and leave me alone!"

Dave put his hand on her arm and asked dryly, "Is that what you'd like me to do?"

"It's not my style to impose myself on anyone. I don't like being where I'm not wanted," Claire answered, her voice unsteady.

She lifted her head and saw the twinkle of mischief in Dave's eyes. "You're making fun of me, aren't you? Oh! I feel so ridiculous . . . I had no idea that you were engaged to Christine!"

"So that's it," said Dave, flatly "And who told you that?"

"Christine, last week. . . ."

"Well, that's the first I've heard of it! A bit strange, wouldn't you say?"

"Everything's a bit strange, Dave. Don't laugh, I don't think it's a bit funny!"

"Well, I do. You have to admit that Christine has an unerring instinct for stirring up trouble and creating dramatic scenes. She's got a great act! Wasn't she roaring off to Megève every day?"

"Yes, in the afternoons."

"She was sitting in a small bar next to the skating rink, directly across the road from the gas station where I always stop to fill up before coming here. She saw me and asked for a ride back."

"Did you know you'd be coming today?" asked Claire, not entirely convinced.

"No, but she was quick enough to take advantage of a situation that would work well with her plans. Believe me, even *I* didn't know I'd be able to get away this weekend. Peter called and very kindly offered to take my place at the hospital. He's not often free, himself. So it's thanks to him that I was able to come."

He took Claire by the arm. "You really aren't much of a psychologist, my dear."

"What do you mean?"

"Can you see Christine being the wife of a country doctor, which, incidentally, is what I want to be? She's a terrific lady and all that, but hardly the type to put up with the unglamorous life that a doctor's wife has to face. On stage, she could probably act the part very well, but in real life she'd last about five minutes!"

"But what if she really loves you? Don't you think that love can change a person?"

"Love, yes, but certainly not infatuation. Now, why don't we forget all this nonsense?"

"All right," agreed Claire, once more beginning to

feel the peaceful contentment she experienced whenever she was in Dave's company.

They walked in silence for a while, just enjoying being with one another. Finally, Dave broke the silence. "So, what have you really been doing for the past two weeks, Claire?"

The real answer was that she'd been spending most of her time waiting for him, but it wasn't the kind of answer she could give him.

"I spent some time exploring the area and I looked through the want ads for a job. Nothing seems too promising, so far. . . ."

"I've been on the lookout for you, too. Do you have any kind of nursing training?"

"Unfortunately, no."

"Will you be able to stay with your old nanny for a while?"

"Yes, she's expecting me back next Tuesday. But I'd really like to find a job as soon as possible . . . oh, isn't that Monique waving at us?"

A group of people was headed their way. A few minutes later, Monique, Philip and Patrick were greeting them with great enthusiasm.

"The snow's a complete mess!" grumbled Philip. "Just like glue!"

"Yes," agreed Monique. "It's really sloppy. If it doesn't freeze tonight, we may as well put away our skis and get out the cards!"

"Hey, I've got an idea!" said Philip with great excitement. "How about spending the day tomorrow at the Saisies Pass?"

The idea met with unanimous approval.

Back at the hotel, they told Marcel of their plans.

"Go ahead, but you'll have to be very careful,"

Marcel said seriously. "Just don't attempt to ski on any slopes that have been in the heat of the sun."

"Why?"

"Because of possible avalanches. Here in Croix-Haute, we have nothing to fear. The slopes aren't steep enough and the snow never gets deep enough, so there's no danger of it all coming down at once. At the Pass, though, it's a different story. Sometimes, even the slightest noise can bring down tons of snow all at once."

"Come with us, then," urged Philip. "You can be our guide."

"I can't tomorrow. I've got some lessons booked. But you'll have Dave with you and he's as good as I am. Remember to take the first-aid kit and always stay together. How many will be going?"

"Five," replied Claire.

"Care to try for six?" Christine had just joined the group. "I just love that kind of outing; with a spice of danger!"

She walked up to Dave and leaned against him, her body moving sinuously, like a cat.

Monique, sensing the suddenly tense atmosphere, quickly announced that she would arrange for the taxis to take them to the Pass, since there was no ski lift to that area.

She was back ten minutes later. Things were getting off to a bad start; no taxis were available until after twelve.

"Then," suggested Marcel, "you can have brunch at eleven and have the whole afternoon to yourselves. Meanwhile, we'd better go and eat. My wife has really outdone herself tonight: the best fondue you've ever tasted!"

Chapter 12

The next day, two taxis pulled up in front of the hotel at precisely noon. When they reached the Pass, they were surprised that the air was not as cold as they expected. But they were delighted to find that the snow was thick and well-packed, quite a change from the snow at Croix-Haute, which had already begun to turn to slush. Dave and Philip decided on the route they would take.

"Look up there ... see that peak, where there's a half-covered chalet? To the right is a trail that leads to the little wood, just farther up. It's not a steep climb Take your time and pace yourselves. We'll meet just at the edge of the wood, on the other side of the mountain, and then start our descent. Now, remember, don't shout, don't call out to each other. We don't want to take any chances."

Everyone was enthusiastic, but before long, Christine was trailing behind and the other two women slowed down to wait for her.

"Talk about your average tortoise!" exclaimed Monique. "You're never going to be able to keep up! Did you really have to wear those tight pants again?"

"How can you two walk so fast?" panted Christine. "I'm exhausted, and it's so hot, climbing."

"Why don't you do the same as we've done?" asked Claire. "Take off your jacket and tie it round your waist."

"But it looks so unattractive hanging round your middle like that! I think I'll just keep mine on."

"Go ahead and cook, if that's what you want," said Monique unsympathetically.

When they finally caught up with the men, they discovered that Dave had gone on ahead.

Claire's skiing was progressing quite well. Her solo outings of the previous weeks had toned up her muscles and she was in fairly good shape. Monique, who had been studying all week, was short of breath. She suggested that Claire go ahead and not wait for her. She and Christine would catch up with the rest of them later.

Claire joined up with Dave just on the other side of the wood. He was looking worried, a small frown wrinkling his tanned forehead.

"At least two miles exposed to the sun. We'll have to get a move on," he said quietly. "I just hope Christine can keep up." Then he leaned toward Claire and smiled. "Not too tired?"

"A little, but I'm fine. Which way do you think we should go?"

"See that boulder over there, sticking its nose out of the snow like a huge shark? We'll go around that and head for the sheepfold, just below, between those two peaks. . . . What on earth is keeping the rest of them?"

"They were right behind me," said Claire. "But it's so hot, they probably stopped to rest for a moment."

There was a feeling of menace in the air. It was subtle, but nevertheless definitely there. Was it due to the utter silence that hung over the mountain? Claire found the sensation eerie and looked around for the others. Then she pointed to a spot in the forest. "Look, Dave, down there! See, in the trees . . . it's them. They must have taken the wrong path."

The rest of the group was some hundred and fifty feet below where Dave and Claire were now standing.

"They must have lost our tracks," he said. "They'll have to cut across the slope to reach us."

Christine, standing a little apart from the others, was gaily waving her poles. "Hello, up there! Hey, Dave! For once, I'm ahead of you!" she shrieked at the top of her lungs.

Claire had turned, fascinated by the enormous overhang of snow above them. Now, an invisible hand seemed to be inking a black line, very slowly, right across the entire mass.

Dave turned white. Grabbing Claire by the arm, he pulled her along with him. "Hurry! Head straight for the sheepfold!" he said urgently, but keeping his voice low. Pushing themselves as hard as they could with their poles, they launched themselves down the hill in a mad dash. Behind them echoed an ear-splitting rumble.

Claire saw Dave indicating to her to raise her arms above her head. The last thing she saw was a flash of red as Christine moved away from the wood. Then the snow knocked her off her feet and she was buried.

The cold brought her around. She opened her eyes

to a translucent world. The snow prevented her making any kind of movement, except for her head, which she could move only slightly in the pocket of air that had been formed by her upthrown arms.

Her first thought was of Dave. Had he been hurt? How could she get to him?

She wasn't sure what position her body was in. Her right hand was still clutching her pole above her head, and cautiously, she tried moving it back and forth. Gradually, she succeeded in wiggling it a few inches.

Her skis were still attached to her boots, rendering her feet immobile. Using all her strength, she managed to move one hand and free her arm. The effort exhausted her, and it was becoming difficult to breathe; her head was beginning to pound. In one last desperate effort, she struggled frantically to move her body and free herself from the enveloping white death.

Then, a large hole appeared above her . . . the sky! She could actually see the sky! And there was Dave, desperately pushing away the snow that had trapped her.

"Claire! Oh, my God, Claire! Can you hear me? Are you all right?"

He freed her legs. One ski had been broken, and he unfastened the skis and helped her up.

She felt something warm trickling down her neck. When she put up her hand to touch it, it came away covered in blood.

Dave examined the wound carefully. "One of your poles must have hit your head as you fell. Does it hurt much? It seems to be only superficial, but it's bleeding quite a lot."

Claire was still trembling from head to foot from

fright, but a warm feeling ran through her body. Dave was safe!

"We're still alive thanks to that rock. The avalanche flowed around both sides of it, and we only caught the edge of it."

Their friends were nowhere to be seen. Dave grabbed at the first-aid kit fastened to his belt. It had fallen open and there was very little left in it. There were a few adhesive bandages, however, and a pair of scissors. He took the scissors and cut the hair around the wound, bandaging it as best he could.

"Dave, this is terrible. Where are the others?"

"Fortunately, they were still in the woods," he said as he bandaged her head. "They may have been shaken up, but they certainly weren't caught by the snow."

Suddenly, Claire saw in her mind the picture of the red pants moving away from the trees. It was the last thing she'd seen, and it meant that Christine must have been in an unprotected spot when the avalanche had hit. Dave hadn't seen it. She was down there, somewhere, under the snow.

Urgently, she asked Dave how long a person could survive buried in snow.

"Half an hour . . . maybe more. It depends on how the snow formed whether there's an air pocket around the person's head."

"Dave, we have to hurry! We have to do something. Just before the snow hit me, I saw Christine coming out of the woods, just about at the level of that little chalet."

"Are you sure?"

"Yes, positive."

"Stay here. I can't be sure how serious that head

wound might be. You'll be better off not to move any more than you have to. I'll head for the sheepfold—I might be lucky enough to find something to dig with."

Ignoring Dave's advice to remain behind, Claire began hunting for her broken ski; if she could find it, she'd be able to help Dave. He'd never be able to dig out all that snow on his own.

She poked around in the snow until she felt it. Triumphantly, she pulled out the half ski, put it on, quickly fastened on the other ski and made her way as fast as she could to join Dave, just as he was breaking down the door of the chalet.

"How long has it been since the avalanche?"

"A little less than ten minutes, I think," answered Dave. "There's still time to save her, if we can find the right spot."

"It's right there, I think," said Claire, pointing to a huge pile of snow at the edge of the wood.

They hurried over and Dave started to dig very cautiously with the shovel he had found in the chalet. Claire knelt, probing the snow with her ski. The wound on her head had reopened with the exertion, and was bleeding again.

With growing anxiety, they continued to dig and probe.

"Dave! She's over here! Hurry! I've got hold of her jacket!"

In no time, they had freed Christine from what might have been her grave. She was unconscious.

"Help me stretch her out," said Dave. "I'll try artificial respiration."

Dave's efforts were quickly successful. In a very few minutes, Christine opened her eyes.

At that moment, a shout was heard from behind the wall of snow.

"Claire! Dave! Christine! Oh, someone, come quickly."

"Claire, stay with Chris and keep rubbing her. Rub her all over, as briskly as you can, that will warm her up. Someone's in trouble; I'll go over and see what I can do."

He hurried away, climbing over the snow to reach the area protected by fir trees.

After a few minutes of Claire's vigorous massaging, Christine became fully alert, and looked round in bewilderment.

"What happened? What have you got on your head? My God," she added, without waiting for Claire's answer, "I was almost killed! Oh! My God! Dave! Where's Dave?"

"Oh, do be quiet!" Claire said irritably. "Dave saved your life and now he's gone to help the others. Leave him alone!"

"Dave!" screamed Christine. She hadn't heard a word.

"Christine! Stop it!" Claire's voice was sharp and commanding.

Christine opened her mouth to shout again, but glancing at Claire's expression, thought better of it. She sat up and started rubbing her leg, moaning softly.

Dave came out of the wood and slid down next to the two women.

"Are they all right, Dave?"

"Philip and Monique seem to be okay, but Patrick was thrown against a tree and has a broken leg. I'm afraid that he might have hurt his spine, as well. I have to find some kind of board to put him on."

Claire followed him. Her head was hurting, but the thought came to her that for the first time in her life, she was thinking about someone besides herself. She just wanted to help.

The chalet appeared to have fallen into a state of disrepair, and consequently, they managed to tear the door from its hinges without too much trouble. Dave dragged it back to where he had left Patrick. With the others' careful help, he managed to get Patrick onto it.

Claire turned to Christine. "You'd better get up," she said. "We have to keep up with the others."

"I can't," Christine said pathetically. "My foot hurts, and I can't move."

"Loosen your boot," said Claire. "If you have a sprain, I'll bind it up."

"A sprain? You must be joking. I'm sure it's a compound fracture!" moaned Christine.

The ankle was slightly swollen.

"Try to walk. Use your poles for support," Claire said impatiently.

"No way," said Christine. "I'll wait for the rescue sled. Better still, here's Dave. He can carry me."

Dave knelt down and examined Christine's ankle. "It's not serious. Lace your boot as tightly as you can and try to climb over that snowbank. You'll have to hurry. Patrick is starting to worry me...and so is Claire," he added, with a glance in her direction.

"But, Dave darling, it's quite impossible," groaned Christine. "I'll wait for the...."

"I said it wasn't serious," he interrupted her abruptly. "There are people who are much worse off than you. You can thank Claire that we got to you so quickly. If it hadn't been for her, you might not be alive right now."

There was irritation in his voice. Claire heard it and realized at that moment that Christine was no longer a rival.

Once they reached the others, Christine stopped complaining. It was obvious that Patrick was in bad shape and she could sense the hostility of the others toward her. She had been responsible for the whole thing, really. No one talked to her. She followed, silent and subdued, as the group headed for the vast expanse of the plateau near the Pass.

Dave and Claire brought up the rear of the party. He put his arm around her shoulders, helping her along. "You've been great, Claire, and I am very grateful for your help." Then he stopped and turned Claire around to face him. "When I first realized, after the avalanche, that you were nowhere to be seen, I . . . ." He broke off and pulling her toward him, he kissed her gently and lingeringly on the mouth.

He drew away, finally. "Come on," he whispered. "We have to catch up to the others."

Turning to face down the mountain, he added, "Oh, thank heavens, I can see the ski patrol starting up with the rescue team."

And in the distance, Claire saw the antlike figures struggling up the slope toward them.

AT THE HOSPITAL, X rays confirmed that Patrick had a broken femur and a displaced disk. He would have to be in a cast for some months, but he took the news well, relieved that it hadn't been any worse.

After her head had been properly bandaged, Claire was turned over to Dave for observation.

It was getting dark by the time they headed back to the hotel. She wondered if the blow on her head might have affected her mind, but she didn't want to ask Dave, for fear of sounding ridiculous. She had read somewhere that people sometimes regain their memories as a result of a sudden shock. She wished it would work for her, only in reverse. She wanted to block out forever a good many things that were all too clear in her memory.

The car that Dave had borrowed was traveling up the mountain road. He was driving very fast, close to the curb. Claire looked through the window, down . . . down . . . into the black empty space just beyond the edge of the road. She had to close her eyes immediately; the feeling of panic and nausea was even worse than before. She began to choke. Her nails dug into the palms of her hands.

Dave's soft voice startled her. "You can open your eyes, now, we're into the woods."

Resenting, suddenly, his apparent ability to read her mind, she impulsively told a lie. "I was just resting."

"Really? Meanwhile, you were hoping that the vertigo would go away, like some kind of magic, right? I told you before; the only person who can help you get over that is you! Think about what happened today. You have to see that as progress, surely."

"I'm not sure what you mean."

"Well, you showed yourself that you have a lot more courage than you thought. You were the one who saved Christine. You should be proud of yourself.

"I think you'd better stay on at the hotel for a few more days," he went on. "You should stay pretty quiet for a while."

"Sorry, doctor. I have to leave tomorrow night," Claire replied firmly.

"That's out of the question," Dave retorted sternly. "You'll stay if I have to tie you to the bed to keep you there."

"All I need is a good night's sleep. Please don't keep insisting. Even if they are supposed to be doctor's orders, I still wouldn't obey them."

Dave said nothing.

Claire was a little hurt by his silence, but she couldn't follow his advice, nor could she tell him why. She didn't even have enough money to stay one more day at the hotel. The accident had caused problems enough in that direction. How was she going to pay the hospital? And she would have to pay for the ski she'd broken, too, since it was rented. She *had* to find a job!

She looked at Dave and wondered how she could make him understand that she had no choice.

The car started the last climb leading to Croix-Haute. It was completely dark now.

Suddenly, Dave veered sharply to the right and brought the car to a stop at the side of the road. Peering ahead, he gave a slight nod, as though pleased that he had been right about something. Starting very slowly, he drove ahead a short distance, then turned onto a small side road. He turned off the engine and lit a cigarette.

Claire didn't move. There was a palpable tension between them, and it continued to build.

After a moment, Dave put out his cigarette, turned

to her and gently cupping her face in his hands, pulled her close to his cheek. His hands felt warm and comforting against her face. She was enjoying his touch, feeling shivers running through her whole body.

He spoke softly. "I think you're forgetting something. You were released from that hospital into my care, remember. If you must leave tomorrow, well, all right . . . but it will have to be with me."

He hugged her closer to him, forestalling her reply.

"Now, no arguments. My car is quite comfortable and the trip won't be all that bad. We'll be in Paris by late afternoon."

"Dave . . . you are so kind that I don't know how to explain this to you. I would be happy to go with you, stay close to you . . . but what am I going to do in Paris? I have no friends there, I wouldn't even have a place to stay."

"Of course you would. I have friends in Paris. Tomorrow night, we'll arrange for you to be admitted to the clinic of a colleague of mine, so you can rest for a few days. You can leave for Brittany just as soon as I'm sure there won't be any complications from that head injury. You can phone Anne-Marie when we get to Paris."

"But—"

"No 'buts,' either," he interrupted. "You're going to follow doctor's orders and that's that. How do you feel now?" he asked softly.

"Much better."

"Then we'd better be getting back to the hotel. You need your sleep." Taking Claire in his arms again, he kissed her slowly and lingeringly, until Claire felt her whole body was on fire. When, at last, he pulled away, he had a teasing smile on his face. "One for the road," he said.

UNAWARE THAT SHE WAS in Peter's father's clinic, Claire stayed a week. When Dave had taken her there, he had arranged with the staff that she not be told what kind of illnesses were treated there.

When Peter dropped around to see her one day, she simply thought that he had gone out of his way to pay her a visit. In truth, he rarely left the clinic from one day to the next. Claire did not meet Peter's father.

No special tests were done, since it was agreed that they might not show accurate results so soon after her injury.

Dave visited her every evening and at the end of the week, he agreed that she was well enough to make the trip back to Brittany.

Dave was quiet as he drove her to the train station. Before leaving her, he looked at her very seriously. "Claire, I want you to promise me somthing," he said.

"What is it?"

"Give me your word that you'll stay away from that pond. And don't go anywhere near it by yourself. Now please don't misunderstand what I'm saying. I don't mean that there's anything wrong with you. It's just that you still have to work on that idea of yours about water having some sort of a strange hold on you. If you feel . . . I should say, if you *think* you feel the urge to go near the water, get in your car and go for a drive. You can beat this thing, if you really want to."

"All right, Dave, I promise. Will you . . . write to me?"

"You'll be hearing from me," he said, gazing at her

intently. "And, Claire . . . have confidence. Things will work out all right, you'll see."

With screeching brakes, the train pulled into the station.

Dave took Claire in his arms and kissed her. "Goodbye, Claire." Before she could answer, he turned and quickly strode away.

Chapter 13

Since she had got back to Brittany, Claire had been very busy applying for jobs. She had a number of interviews, including several for teaching positions, but the work available outside Paris didn't pay as much as she thought she needed. She was getting to the point, however, where she would have to accept the next job she was offered. Anne-Marie had been willing to lend Claire some money, encouraging her to be selective about the job she accepted.

The minute the mailman opened the gate, Claire would race to meet him. Sitting on the large stone just inside the garden, she would tear open her letters, and her slow, dejected walk back to the house would be enough to tell Anne-Marie that the letters contained merely format replies and rejections. She also knew that Claire was expecting to hear from Dave.

"You'd like him," Claire had told her enthusiastically. "He's tall and has brown eyes. Sometimes he's a little sarcastic, but nanny, he is so kind. And he promised to help me find a job."

Anne-Marie had told her that perhaps she shouldn't rely too much on such promises, and Claire, hurt, had not mentioned Dave's name again.

Why hadn't he written? She was sure that he had felt something more than friendship for her. His warm brown eyes couldn't have been lying . . . could they? Hadn't he held her in his arms and kissed her? She could still feel his warm strong hand touching her cheek, and his mouth on hers.

The memory brought an ache to her heart. Every time she thought about it, she would bury her face sadly in Duke's thick fur. The dog would stay still for a while, then begin to whine a little, and lick her face.

A cold March rain had been pouring down for two days. That afternoon it finally stopped, but the sky remained overcast with lowering clouds. Claire felt very depressed, and even Duke was quiet. He didn't jump for his leash, or pull at Claire's skirt as he usually did.

"Why don't you go out for a walk?" suggested Anne-Marie. "You used to love to walk after a rainstorm."

"I don't feel much like going out, thank you, nanny. It's so cozy in here by the fire, I think I'd rather stay in."

"You'll have all the time in the world for staying in when you're a teacher; why don't you go out and look for spring flowers? If you look hard enough, you're sure to find the first few daffodils of the season."

"There are enough flowers in here already, nanny," replied Claire listlessly. "Besides, my heart isn't in it."

"Dear me! What a thing to say! Do you have to talk like that? You . . ." Anne-Marie began reproachfully.

"You know, nanny, I don't think I look old enough

to be a teacher. What if I put my hair back, in a bun. . . ." Claire walked over to the mirror and pulled back her thick, golden hair, shaping it into a severe bun at the back.

"There!" she said, when she'd finished. She spun around. "Well, nanny, what do you think of my new hairstyle?"

There was a sudden knock on the door. Duke jumped up, barking, and Anne-Marie rose to answer the door.

"Down, Duke! Oh, it's you, Tom!" she said as she stepped aside to bring the visitor into the house. The little boy was red faced and out of breath. "What brings you here?"

"The lady at the post office sent me with a telegram for Miss Claire de Montebourg," answered the boy, as he handed her the envelope.

I wonder if one of the schools has accepted me, thought Claire.

Anne-Marie handed the telegram to Claire, and offered the small boy some of her famous gingerbread in thanks for his long dash from the post office He accepted with alacrity and then disappeared with the same speed at which he arrived.

"You see, nanny? All I had to do was change my hairstyle!" said Claire with a wry smile as she opened the envelope.

There was a pause, and then she cried out, "Nanny, look! Oh, I can't believe it! Here, read it."

"What on earth is it, Claire?" asked Anne-Marie, looking round for her glasses. She took the message and walked over to the window. "My goodness, what a turn of events!"

Claire ran to Anne-Marie and gave her an excited

hug. Excited by all the sudden movement, Duke jumped up and down, barking happily.

"Claire! Stop!" cried Anne-Marie, laughing. "I have to catch my breath. Oh, my! Look at you! I must say, I haven't seen such color in your cheeks for ages."

"Nanny, nanny . . . tell me I'm not dreaming!" As if to assure herself, Claire read the telegram again, aloud. "Arriving St. Quay Thursday, ten a.m. See you then. Dave."

"I never really gave up hope, nanny, and I was right. Now I know that he hasn't forgotten me. I'm so happy . . . and you'll be able to meet him . . . tomorrow."

"So your heart isn't dried up like an old apple after all!" said Anne-Marie, a twinkle in her eye. "I wonder why he's coming all the way to Brittany. It's quite a distance!"

"Maybe he's found a job for me!"

"He could have written to you about it."

"That's true . . . but maybe he wants to talk to me about it, I told him quite a lot about myself, you know. Oh, nanny! Don't look like that. I get the distinct feeling that there's something about this that you don't like at all."

"No, that's not true, Claire," answered Anne-Marie with a smile. "But you see, in my day, young women were not nearly so free with young men. I'm sure I'll never get used to it, that's all."

"Do you really think that young girls behaved any better when you were young?" Claire retorted. "We're just more open about our feelings nowadays, and we're not any worse than all of you were in your day! Now, we have to decide what to have for lunch tomorrow. Could we have that lovely fish dish of yours? And some ham and cheese crepes. I'll pay you back for all this, darling nanny, just as soon as I start working!"

The next morning, Claire awakened to the first sounds of spring. The birds had returned from warmer southern climes, and were chirping outside her window as if to announce to her the advent of the new season. Claire lay in bed for a few minutes wondering at the cause of her feeling of excited anticipation. Then she remembered: Dave was coming.

She thanked heaven for the glorious day, and scrambled out of bed to begin her preparations for the guest's arrival.

As she combed her hair over the wound that was now almost healed, she thought idly that Dave had never seen her wearing anything but ski pants. Today she would wear a honey-colored, light wool suit, which, she knew, enhanced the fine lines of her body.

Claire was ready hours before Dave was expected. "Would you like me to set the table for lunch, nanny?" she asked, eager for something to keep herself occupied.

"Before breakfast? You must be joking. Why don't you just sit down and read a book, or something. Or go outside; it's going to be a lovely day."

Claire had a small breakfast, and then helped Anne-Marie with the sweeping and dusting. Then, unable to contain herself any longer, she said, "Maybe I should go out to the road and meet him. I could be at the highway in no time, and that's the only possible way he could come."

She put on the jacket to her suit and started out of the house.

Duke jumped to his feet and followed her; the sight of her putting on a jacket and changing her shoes meant a walk in the countryside, and this morning there were all kinds of new and enticing scents to explore.

Claire stopped and patted the dog. "Good boy, not this time. You're going to have to stay with nanny."

Duke sat down, dejected. He didn't understand why he wasn't wanted. His eyes were so sad, Claire put her arm round his neck and lightly kissed his head.

"I'm sorry, Duke. Next time, I promise."

She took a few steps. Obstinately, the dog got up and followed her again.

"Nanny!" called Claire. "Would you mind taking Duke? Dave might not like animals, and anyway Duke will get the inside of his car all dirty."

Anne-Marie grabbed the dog and took him inside. As the door closed behind him, Duke let out a long, mournful howl.

Claire walked quickly and soon reached the ruins of the old abbey that overlooked the highway.

She thought of how marvelous it would be to see Dave again, imagining every detail of what was going to happen when they actually met. He would take her in his arms and . . . .

Feeling herself flushing with excitement, she ran the rest of the way and sat down on the guard rail, quite out of breath. She could see the main highway for quite a distance, and started to worry: Dave had said that he would be there by ten, and it was nearly ten-thirty. What could be keeping him? An accident? Had the car broken down?

Claire suddenly had a terrible feeling that some-

thing awful had happened to him. She remembered
the dog's howl and a shiver went through her. Her
imagination conjured up a dreadful accident . . . Dave
was hurt, even dead, perhaps.

She decided to return to the house. Very slowly, her
feet dragging, she started down the road. She was
subdued, much of her earlier high spirits having
evaporated in the anticlimax of his not arriving and her
apprehension that something may have happened to
him.

When she reached the narrow sideroad that led
from the house to the pond, she saw the gates wide
open and the familiar gray car parked in the yard.

She gasped, feeling a great outpouring of relief, and
dashed toward the house.

As she ran up the path, Dave came out, followed by
Anne-Marie.

"Ah! Here she is! I was just coming to find you!
Good morning, Claire!"

He smiled and took her hand, his dark eyes sparkling with happiness.

"Dave! I'm so glad to see you. I . . . I thought you'd
had an accident."

"Why would you think a thing like that? Of course
not. I've just come from Brest, where I dropped off a
friend. I got a bit lost and ended up here, quite by
chance, on some unknown backroad! Here, let me
look at you. Claire, you look marvelous!"

He was still holding her hand, and Claire, trembling
with emotion and sudden shyness, just looked at him,
at a loss for words. Dave was even more attractive than
she'd remembered, and his voice—she'd forgotten—
deep and gentle.

"I was here right on time," he continued, "and I

haven't wasted a minute. Anne-Marie and I have been getting to know one another, and now we're well on the way to becoming old friends. I've made Duke's acquaintance, too," he added, patting the dog affectionately.

Anne-Marie was wearing her velvet dress and her finest embroidered headdress. She smiled and nodded her head. "I've put David to use already, Claire. He got the water from the well for me, and if he had had his way, he'd have set the table, too. Come inside and have some wine, you two. We'll have an early lunch. David, you must be famished."

Anne-Marie had outdone herself. Her fish and stuffed crepes were just like those created by the finest chefs in Paris. Everything was delicious.

Dave ate with great enthusiasm, but Claire just played with her food; excitement and nervousness had taken away her appetite. She was overjoyed to see Dave again but also curious to know if he had found a job for her. Trying to find out without asking directly, she casually mentioned, in the course of conversation, that she had applied for several jobs as a teacher.

"I didn't know you liked children," Dave remarked, looking at her.

"Yes, I do, very much. And I like the thought of teaching those young minds something worthwhile. . . . The only thing that scares me is standing up in front of a whole classroom of children. I just wonder if I would be able to control them."

Dave's laughter startled the dog, who had just dozed off. Duke still hadn't quite forgiven Claire for leaving him behind that morning, and was lying on Dave's foot: Duke appeared to have taken an instant liking to him.

"Why don't we go for a walk?" Dave proposed, after they had finished their coffee. "I see there's a wood just behind the house. Is there a pair of rubber boots I could borrow?"

"Yes, by all means," said Anne-Marie. "I'll stay here, I think, and clean up. No, you can't help, go and enjoy the sun. I'll tie up Duke, so he won't be bothering you."

"Tie the poor fellow up on a day like this?" protested Dave. "Here, Duke, show me where your leash is."

Duke leaped high in the air, trying to reach Dave's shoulders and lick his face, to show his appreciation.

For a time, they walked along in silence, with Duke sniffing ecstatically in the undergrowth. No matter how happy Claire was to be with Dave, she knew only too well that he would be here only for a very short time, and her happiness was marred by the anticipation of the moment he would have to leave.

She sighed. Dave, who had been watching her covertly, finally spoke. "You don't seem too happy, Claire. Are you worrying about getting a job?"

"I don't want to think about that just now, Dave. I just want to enjoy having you here."

"Well, you could've fooled me—you look so glum!"

A large birch tree that had been cut down was lying at the side of the road. They sat next to each other on the smooth, white trunk, warming themselves in the sun.

"How are you, really, Claire? Have you had any trouble with that wound since you left Paris?"

"No, none at all," she replied. "I forget about it except when I brush my hair."

"Have you gone anywhere near the pond when you've been out walking?"

"No. Besides, I gave you my word that I wouldn't."

"Do you want to go to the pond . . . now, with me?"

The answer came instantly. "No!"

She felt that Dave was moving far away from her and her heart skipped a beat. "Dave, you don't seem to understand! Why should I put myself in a position where I would just be humiliated in front of you all over again? You know very well that I'm not cured! I had hoped that the avalanche would have . . . but . . . ."

"That's too bad," said Dave. "Your life might take an entirely different direction if only you could become a little more reasonable."

"I consider myself to be quite reasonable," Claire answered stiffly.

Dave put his arm around her waist, and kissed her, feeling her gradually relax in his arms. "Which would you prefer," he asked after he released her. "To teach some thirty children, or to look after one small boy—who is really quite bright—and spend your time with a charming older woman who in no time at all would be your very good friend? I might also add that the pay would be at least twice as much as you could expect to get, teaching in a state school."

Claire had been listening with amazement. "Are you serious?" she asked. "Where does this woman live? Oh, I'd love to have a job like that! I'd take it in a minute! I told you about the qualms I've had about teaching a whole class!"

Suddenly, she had the feeling that a whole new future was opening up for her.

"Gently, now, Claire; don't get carried away. It's Aunt Suzanne and Simon I'm talking about. You remember them? Since you met Simon, he hasn't got any better. His father and Peter and I all decided that some fresh sea air might possibly help him. So Aunt Suzanne is going to take him to Ouessant—do you know it? It's a tiny island—only four miles long by two and a half miles wide—just off the coast of Brittany. A friend of ours has very kindly agreed to lend us his house there. It's called 'Ty Breitz'. But Aunt Suzanne needs someone to help her with Simon, and to help him with his lessons while he's there. I've talked to them about you, and they think it's a great idea. What do you think?"

"Oh, wonderful!" cried Claire. "I really liked Simon, even in the short time I saw him, and I'm sure your Aunt Suzanne and I would get on splendidly! She seemed so warm and loving. Dave, I'd go to the end of the earth, if need be. You don't realize how happy it makes me to know that I won't have to teach a whole class of children. I was terrified at the thought!"

"Claire, just stop and think for a moment. Have you considered the fact that an island is surrounded by water, and this particular island is a five-hour boat trip from the mainland."

Claire didn't say a word. She frowned, thinking. After a pause, she asked hesitantly, "Dave, you mentioned once that there was a test to scan brain waves. If I took a test like that, do you think that a treatment to cure me might be found? I told you before I was willing to go along with the tests . . . even an operation, if you think it would help."

Dave hugged her close to him; her expression revealed her inner torment, but there was also the faintest hint of hope, deep in her eyes.

"Claire, I've told you time and time again that, if you really wanted to be cured, you would be. And this testing would be the first step. You remember the clinic where I took you to rest after the accident. They have that sort of equipment, and you could also be treated there, if the tests showed anything. I'll take you with me tomorrow, if you like. We'll know very soon if there's any problem. But the decision has to be yours, Claire, and only yours. It's very important that you understand that your job with Simon will depend on the results."

"Dave . . . I'm very grateful for your concern. And of course I'll go with you," Claire said, her face bright with happiness.

He looked at her. Sunlight played in her hair, picking out streaks of gold. All around them, the forest stood in friendly silence; the only sound to be heard was a bird calling from somewhere above them.

Claire leaned her head against Dave's shoulder and felt the rough texture of his jacket against her cheek. She closed her eyes, the better to fully savor this moment of blissful contentment.

For several minutes, neither of them moved. Then slowly, Dave lifted Claire's lips to his and he kissed her, first gently then with a passion Claire had only dreamed of. His arms tightened around her, and Claire responded with an ardor matching his.

She drew away from him a little, all the while looking into his eyes. "Dave . . . " she murmured in a tremulous voice.

"Don't say anything," Dave said gently, putting a

finger on her lips. "Let it be enough, for the moment, that we're close to each other. Sometimes words complicate things and are much better left unsaid."

"Dave, this time I want you to listen to me," said Claire vehemently. "I know that you think I'm egotistical and maybe even a little arrogant. Well, I used to be all those things, I guess. But since meeting you, I've begun to learn that happiness comes from concern for others, and not myself. I want you to understand that I . . . ."

He stopped her by covering her mouth with his. He kissed her for a long minute, then took her face in both his hands, holding it gently as though it were a precious object, and looked at her lovingly.

"Claire," he said in a low voice, "our paths crossed at a time when solitude and despair were getting the better of you, and I was able to help you a little. You're not really clinging to me, you're clinging to the doctor who saved you from yourself. You don't really know me, or even yourself, well enough yet."

There was profound tenderness in his voice. His hands caressed her face, softly, and Claire could feel the slight tremble in his fingers.

"You are so beautiful, Claire. . . . Now, we must go back," he said suddenly.

He got up quickly and called to Duke who had been dozing in the sun.

So that's it, Claire thought to herself. *He thinks I've got a crush, a patient-doctor thing . . . some kind of whim of an emotionally unstable person.*

She watched Dave as he played with Duke. A sudden thought stabbed at her heart. *What if he's in love with someone else, and is just letting me down gently?*

Quickly, Claire discarded the idea, and decided resolutely to change so drastically that Dave would no longer have any reason to doubt that her feelings for him were true.

Chapter 14

They left the next day, Claire promising Anne-Marie that she would be back in two days. To save her needless worry, Claire and Dave had agreed not to say anything about the clinic. Anne-Marie thought Claire was going to Paris for a job interview, and returning by train the day after next.

Sitting in Dave's car, Claire took one last look back at the little house, then turned in her seat to look ahead, feeling that a whole new life was about to begin for her. They were silent for a long time before Claire spoke.

"Dave, you've never told me much about yourself. Peter mentioned that you share an apartment with him, but that's about all I know about you!"

"That's right. We have an apartment in a drafty old house, and we have a part-time housekeeper, who tries to keep the place in some reasonable order."

"What do you do in your free time . . . besides ski, I mean?"

"I don't seem to have much free time," he laughed.

"My patients keep me much too busy. There's usually so much work to do that I never seem to have enough time even to sleep."

They chatted away easily about Dave's busy life, breaking off every now and then to exclaim at the passing sights.

In no time, it seemed to Claire, Dave told her that they were almost there. He parked the car in the lot reserved for staff only and the two of them walked into the clinic.

Before leaving her in her room to go back to his patients, Dave urged her to get as much rest as she could. Sensing her anxiety, he explained that the process consisted basically of recording the brain waves; the lines would indicate precisely the nature of the problem, if any, and exactly where the problem was located.

Although she made every effort to stay calm, every sound made Claire jump. Even the noise of a door being opened or closed somewhere down the hall caused her to start. That evening a young doctor came by, and after hearing her describe her symptoms, escorted her through the clinic to the room where the testing would be done.

Passing a room where the door was ajar, Claire thought she saw Peter, wearing a white smock, talking to a nurse. She had thought he worked at one of the large hospitals, and was puzzled to see him here. Most likely just someone who looks like him, she thought.

She was escorted into a room filled with all kinds of sophisticated electronic equipment. The door was closed behind her and she was left alone. The room was totally quiet, and Claire wondered if, for some reason, it had been specially insulated.

After a few minutes, two white-coated assistants came in. Claire was shown to a comfortable chair, not unlike a dentist's chair, and the two men busied themselves attaching small electrodes to various places on her head. These electrodes, in turn, were connected to a console, the surface of which was covered with mass of buttons, lights and dials.

Looks like the control panel of a jet, thought Claire, trying to cheer herself up and not totally succeeding. *I feel exactly like a criminal who's been condemned to the electric chair. . . .*

"Try to relax," suggested one of the assistants, kindly. "Try not to think about anything. Now, just close your eyes. . . ."

He had Claire open and close her eyes about twenty times. She had to breathe very deeply, then normally, and finally not at all. Then, she had to stare at a flashing red light without blinking. The concentration produced a dull pain behind her eyes.

The data sheet rolled out of the console; six writing rods traced lines on the continuously moving paper and the two assistants bent over it, deciphering the tracings. From time to time, one of them would make a mark on the sheet with a red pencil, and Claire could feel her anxiety increase. What were they finding? What did the marks mean? Were the family illnesses being exposed to the scrutiny of these strangers? She was so relieved that Dave wasn't there.

The muscles of her neck felt knotted, and her shoulders sagged as though leaden.

"Is the director here yet?" one of the assistants asked the other.

"Yes, but he's in surgery. We'll have to wait because

he wants to do this diagnosis himself, for some reason."

Is it really that serious, thought Claire wildly. *Why else should the head of a clinic want to involve himself?*

"That's all, thank you, Miss de Montebourg. All finished. Now, it wasn't all that bad, after all, was it?"

Back in her bright little room, Claire agonized and fretted. Soon she would have the answer to what was wrong with her. . . . What exactly would she learn about herself? Would they, in fact, tell her the truth if her illness were really serious?

A nurse knocked on the door, interrupting Claire's troubled thoughts. She led Claire to a large, airy office, indicated a chair for Claire to sit in, then withdrew.

Two doctors stood with their backs to Claire, talking in subdued tones to a third person whom Claire couldn't see. She could only hear the serious tone in his deep, authoritarian voice.

The two doctors left a minute or two later, and the third doctor, seated behind a large desk, beckoned to Claire. She was pale and trembling.

"Please sit down, Miss de Montebourg."

Almost paralyzed with fright, she sat down again, this time in a chair facing the desk, and looked at the doctor in front of her. The man had iron-gray hair, and the eyes in his energetic, lined face, were the color of steel. She'd never be able to hide anything from this man . . . he seemed to be able to see right through her.

For a while, it seemed as though he had forgotten Claire's presence entirely as he went through the notes which the two doctors had left with him. He then went over the sheet on which Claire had seen the lines being traced. Slowly and carefully, he examined every inch of the paper. Finally, he folded the sheet and put it on the desk, looking at Claire.

"How are you feeling?" he asked.

Claire opened her mouth to answer, but no words came out.

"Why are you trembling?" he asked, gently, but again, she was unable to answer.

The doctor got up, walked around the desk and sat down on an easy chair, which he pulled up close to hers. "I want to speak to you, but first I want you to try to relax," he said firmly. "I want you to listen to what I'm going to say: it's important."

She concentrated on breathing slowly and deeply, and felt her heartbeat gradually resume its normal rhythm. The doctor smiled and went back to sit behind his desk.

"How long have you been having these dizzy spells?"

Claire looked up at him in quick surprise. She didn't remember saying anything about dizzy spells to the doctor who had questioned her.

"I've always been afraid of empty spaces, they've always made me dizzy . . . as long as I can remember."

"Many people are, but nobody thinks of them as symptoms of mental illness. Now, tell me, when was it that you first began to feel these symptoms get worse?"

"When I learned that some members of my family had committed suicide," Claire replied at once.

"And who told you?"

Claire hesitated. She was embarrassed at having to tell him that she'd been eavesdropping and had overheard a conversation between a maid and a laundry woman. But she just couldn't lie with those eyes boring into her.

"I heard a conversation between two members of our household staff," she answered, blushing.

"Well, I think you've probably been punished for doing that far more seriously than you deserved. What you've done is convince yourself that you're mentally disturbed. You were highly-strung, probably feeling alienated from your family, capable of sudden bursts of anger. . . . Am I right, so far?"

"Yes."

"Then, when you heard that conversation, the shock could have created a neurosis that might have had terrible consequences. Now I want you to listen to me very carefully. There's nothing organically wrong with you. The results of the tests we've just done prove that beyond the shadow of a doubt. Your graph is completely normal, without a trace of abnormal brain activity. I hope that that will reassure you."

"But the dizzy spells go back to long before I heard the conversation," protested Claire, "and . . . and I know that they're not my imagination."

"They have some basis in your psychic self . . . fear perhaps. Or they may have something to do with your migraine, which I notice you told the other doctor you suffered from. Often you'll suffer the symptoms of a migraine coming on, and then it won't, for some reason, develop any further. Believe me," he said as he got up, "you are perfectly healthy. Just try to avoid anything that might increase your anxiety. You are highly-strung and fretful by nature, but as time goes on, through sheer self-discipline, you'll be able to conquer the phobias you have."

Claire wasn't convinced. Certainly, the doctor sounded sincere, but surely her cure wasn't as simple as mind over matter. Perhaps she could get another opinion. . . .

She got up to leave and turned to thank the doctor, when he walked up to her and put his hands on her shoulders. He looked at her for a moment and then smiled. When he spoke, his voice was much more friendly. "You're not convinced, are you? I can see it. Well, let me ask you this—do you think I would leave my child in your care, if I thought there was the slightest chance you might be mentally ill? You're going to be the one to take on some of the responsibility for the education and welfare of my son, Simon. David suggested you for the job, and you seem to be a very responsible young woman. You have the full support of Suzanne Chanoy, too," he added.

Claire was stunned. Her thoughts were awhirl. But there were more surprises in store for her.

The doctor took her by the arm and walked her to the door as he continued. "It was at my request that Dave said nothing to you. I advised him not to say a word about who this clinic belonged to, in case it upset you and prejudiced you either against the tests, or about helping Simon."

He stopped and looked at her intently. "And for what it's worth, David told me he didn't believe there was anything the least bit wrong with you. We'll meet again very shortly. I'll be at Milhouse on Sunday with Peter, my elder son, whom I believe you've met already. I hope that my boisterous second son will be on his best behavior. Goodbye for now, Miss de Montebourg. Rest here until tomorrow, and remember what I told you."

DAVE PICKED CLAIRE UP the next morning. Surprised at herself, she had had a good night's sleep, and felt much better. Dave didn't mention anything about the tests or their results, but suggested that he take her immediately to Milhouse. She agreed happily.

They drove for a long time without speaking.

Claire glanced sideways at Dave's strong profile. She wanted so much to reach up and touch his face, run her fingers through his thick black hair. She remembered how hesitant and distant she'd been before and wondered at the change in herself.

Dave stared straight ahead, frowning. A deep wrinkle creased his forehead.

Finally, Claire broke the silence. "Dave, did you see Doctor . . . Peter's father?"

"Dr. Breveley. Yes, I saw him," he answered, without turning his head. "And he confirmed what I've been thinking all along. Now you don't have to worry anymore. It's simply a question of will and determination on your part."

The words were spoken without expression; an answer given because a question was asked. Dave seemed very far away. . . . Scenery flashed by and Claire didn't notice; she and Dave were about to part, and already their closeness was disappearing. Dave had told her that Simon was expected to stay on the island for about six months. How could she hope that he would still be thinking of her when she got back?

I'm going to lose him, she thought despairingly.

"Claire, are you sure you know what you're doing?" Dave's serious voice interrupted her thoughts.

"Yes, quite sure. Why?"

"No regrets about having made the decision to take on the thankless job of being a teacher? There's still time, you know, to turn around and go back to your family, where you can get on with your studies. . . ."

"And leave Aunt Suzanne in the lurch, with a sick boy, and a strange house?" Claire retorted. "A nice way to thank Dr. Breveley for everything he did for me at the clinic!"

She paused for a moment and then went on a little more calmly. "I've given this move a great deal of thought, Dave, and am confident in my decision . . . at peace with it. At some later date, I may choose to finish my studies at the Law Faculty, but I'll cross that bridge when I come to it. Right now, I'm accomplishing two things, helping Simon . . . and helping myself."

A spark of admiration flashed in Dave's eyes. "Then why have you been so worried ever since we left Paris?"

Claire didn't answer.

"Don't you want to talk about it?" Dave persisted. "In a short while, we're going to have to leave each other."

Still she remained silent.

Dave glanced in her direction and saw that she had lowered her head, the gleaming brown curtain of her hair hiding her face, and the tears that were on it. He spoke again, his voice very soft. "Claire, listen to me. I'm not going to forget you; I'll write as often as I can. But if you don't hear from me for a time, just remember that it's my work, and nothing else, that's preventing me from writing. You've got a challenge ahead of you, both in Simon and in yourself. I'm not worried about the fact that there'll be water all around you, but I'm still a little concerned about those dizzy spells and what might be causing them."

"Is that the good doctor talking?" Claire asked as

Dave pulled up in front of Aunt Suzanne's house and turned off the ignition.

"No, this time it's the friend," he said. "I'll try to get some time off in a couple of months, and spend a few days with you, but I can't promise. I'll let you know closer to the time."

Claire's heart was as quick to hope as it had been to doubt. She felt strong again, and equal to the test their separation would provide for the deep feelings she had for him. There was a smile on her face as Dave leaned over to kiss her, deeply, passionately, holding her in an embrace so warm and secure Claire didn't ever want to be released. . . .

AUNT SUZANNE CAME OUT to greet them. She welcomed Claire warmly, and said that she was delighted that Claire had agreed to take this job.

Dave remained silent, while Aunt Suzanne and Claire greeted each other. When they had finished, he gave a perfunctory kiss on the cheek to them both, and promising to keep in touch he got back into his car and drove off, his wheels screeching.

Chapter 15

Suzanne Chanoy was aware that Claire was going through some kind of emotional upheaval; moreover, she was aware that this was Claire's first job and she had no previous experience. Aunt Suzanne took it all in her stride; she was a naturally warm and affectionate woman, and to some extent viewed Claire as her protégée as well as a surrogate daughter. Her welcome to Claire had been especially warm.

Fighting back the tears at Dave's departure, Claire walked into the house that was to be her home until they moved to the island. Aunt Suzanne continued past her into the kitchen to see Marie.

Turning, Claire almost bumped into Simon, who had been standing behind her. Claire smiled. "Hello, Simon. Do you remember me?"

"Hello. Yes," he said, his gaze unwavering. "You look like the Red Knight."

"Do I? And who is the Red Knight?" she asked in amusement.

"He's in a painting. I'll show him to you. There are two knights in it and the red one looks just like you."

She took his hand, a little surprised to feel how frail it was. They went into the kitchen together.

"I see that you two have already met again," said Aunt Suzanne. "I'll show you to your room, Claire," she continued, rising from her chair. "Make yourself at home for the few days you're here. We'll be leaving next week, I hope you don't mind too much that we'll be going to such a remote area?"

"I don't know it at all," answered Claire. "But it'll be fun living on an island—I hear this one is lovely. I remember a trip to the Isle of Man, off the coast of England, when I was much younger, which I loved. Now, am I to begin working with Simon before we leave?"

"No," replied the little boy with great determination.

"Of course you're going to have to do some work," said his aunt. "You'll start on Monday. At first, Claire, his lessons will have to be very short. As he begins to feel better, we can prolong them, little by little. Here's your room. I do hope you like it."

Claire walked into a room flooded with sunlight. The furniture was plain, but very comfortable-looking. The large window overlooked an orchard, a beautiful sight for all the trees were in blossom.

Aunt Suzanne took Claire's hands in her own. "We won't be staying here very long, but till we leave for the island I want you to make Milhouse your home. Next week, we'll put up with the inconveniences together, but while you're here, in my house, I want you to feel as comfortable as you would in your own home. Now, I must leave you and see to some things downstairs," she added, sensing Claire's rising emotion. "Come on, Simon, Claire will join us later in the living room, after she's had a rest."

"Aunt Suzanne," Claire said, a little shyly, as the older woman was turning away with Simon to leave Claire alone. "There is something I must ask you. May I use your telephone for a minute? I . . . told my nanny . . . I mean, er, Anne-Marie Leduc is expecting me to return to Brittany. I'd like to send her a telegram, I'm staying with her, you see, or at least, I was. . . ."

"Do whatever you want, Claire dear. Please make this house your own. The telephone is in the living room downstairs. Listen, dear, do you need to go back home to get your baggage, or what? I haven't a car, I'm afraid; I just depend on one of the boys to give me a ride when I have to go somewhere."

"Please, Mrs. Ch— I mean, Aunt Suzanne; don't worry about me. Honestly, I'm fine. But I should let nanny know where I am."

Claire followed Suzanne Chanoy downstairs, but went into the living room instead of continuing into the kitchen. She explained in the telegram that she was at Milhouse and that Dave had got her a job and she was needed right away. She also asked Anne-Marie to pack up the bare minimum of clothing—jeans and sweaters, and send them directly on to the address at Ashant, the local name of the island where they would be going. Claire finished the message with a promise to write as soon as possible.

After relaying the contents of the telegram over the phone, Claire went up to her bedroom to unpack her overnight case. But before she did so, she sank down onto the soft bed and looked around her. It wasn't a grand room, but she smiled wryly to herself as she recalled Aunt Suzanne's words about being as comfortable as she would in her own home. How much more secure she felt in this plain, simple room than she had in her own grand, ornate room at the château in Neuilly!

THE FOLLOWING MONDAY, when the time came for Simon's lessons, the little boy was nowhere to be found.

Assuming that there must be any number of places in the rambling old farmhouse where a little boy could hide, Claire went through all the rooms on the main floor, but without success. Then she thought of the attic, remembering the third floor of her parents' house, and her private room up there.

The attic at Milhouse was vast, and determinedly she began at one end a systematic search—behind cardboard boxes, between pieces of dusty, dilapidated furniture. It was as Claire began to look through a rack of old clothes, that she saw his head. Saying nothing immediately, she just smiled—partly in relief at having found him, and partly because his smile was so disarming that the irritation she had felt evaporated.

"Simon!" Claire said finally, with no trace of censure in her voice. "What about your lesson? Your aunt sent you to the library, not the attic!"

"Well . . . yes, I know," he said, "But the attic's so much more interesting than the library. Come and look!"

There was a large painting lying at the bottom of a trunk. Claire saw the knight, dressed in a red cape, pulling a sword from a stone in the middle of a stream. A second knight stood on the bank, watching him. The artist had given the young knight in red a handsome face with brown eyes and golden curls. The colors were still quite bright, even though the paint had begun to peel in places.

Sir Galahad and Sir Percival, thought Claire.

"I told you that he looked like you," said Simon. "I'd really like to take it out, but Marie told me not to even open any of the trunks." He looked down at his feet, shuffling them a little.

"Well, in that case, you really shouldn't have opened it, then, should you?" asked Claire, putting on as stern an expression as she could muster. She took Simon by the hand and marched him out of the attic.

"Come along," she said. "We have work to do!"

Looking very unhappy, Simon settled himself at his little desk a short while later. Not a sound came out of his mouth when Claire asked him to read. His mute-ness irritated her; Claire knew perfectly well that Simon could read.

I don't know the first thing about becoming a teacher, she thought to herself, a little discouraged. *How do you get a stubborn child like Simon to do what you ask?*

Claire decided to try a different approach. "If you do well, I'll tell you the story of the painting."

The little boy's eyes lit up. "Do you know it?" he asked eagerly.

"I know it quite well. It's the story of King Arthur and the Knights of the Round Table. If you get your work done in good time, I'll tell you about some of their adventures every day."

Immediately, Simon's attitude changed. He was quite a studious child, by nature, and Claire was delighted at his intelligence.

By the end of the morning, they were the best of friends.

THAT WEEK, EVERY ROOM in the place was cluttered with boxes as Aunt Suzanne packed for their stay on the island. It was a time-consuming, exhausting job, and she asked Claire to look after Simon at meals and at bedtime.

Meals were the worst part. No matter what she did, Claire couldn't get him to eat more than a mouthful. She tried bribing, scolding... nothing worked. At their first meal together, it took almost an hour to get him to drink a glass of orange juice.

Patience may be a virtue, thought Claire, but there's a limit to everything. What do you do to make a child eat, when he isn't hungry?'

She took the boy to his room without a further word. Simon looked at her unhappily, and took as long as possible to undress himself.

Claire watched him in silence, her anger fading rapidly. The child was so desperately thin—he was a mass of angles and protrusions. Not one part of his delicate frame was properly filled out. Claire's heart went out to him.

Simon, a highly sensitive child, immediately caught the change in her expression. Sensing that this was the time to ask forgiveness, he went to her. "Don't be mad at me," he said in a small voice. "Tomorrow, I'll really try to eat."

"Yes, but tonight you've upset a lot of people. Besides, how do you expect to grow up big and strong like your brother, or Uncle Dave, if you don't eat?"

"But I'm just not hungry," replied Simon, his head drooping.

He was having some difficulty with the buttons on his pajama top and Claire took him onto her knee. Simon put his sticklike arms around her neck and kissed her on the cheek. She was moved by the little boy's spontaneous gesture of affection and kissed him back. When the child finally fell asleep, she was smiling, and so was he.

A FEW DAYS LATER, the household awaited the arrival of Dr. Breveley. He was bringing with him the nurse, Claudette Ramon, who was going to look after Simon's health. Peter, who was going to drive the travelers to the boat, would be coming as well, in his own car. He had also promised to go over to the island with them, to see that everything was in order at the rented house, but he was flying rather than traveling by boat.

At noon, the phone rang.

When Aunt Suzanne picked it up, she recognized Dave's voice.

"Hello, Dave. . . . Yes, we're all packed; we're just waiting for the two Brevelys and the nurse. . . . Of course, hang on a minute, she's right here. . . . Good-bye, Dave. . . . Yes, you take care of yourself, too. Claire," she added, holding out the receiver. "Dave wants to talk to you."

Too busy to get away, Dave had called to wish her bon voyage and a safe trip. He had also remembered that today was her birthday, and perhaps that fact, more than anything else, gave her pleasure. The bond between them was growing . . . she could feel it. The separation was going to be a long one. . . .

As Claire was going along the upstairs landing to her bedroom, Aunt Suzanne called to her from her own room. She took Claire by the hand and smiled.

"I didn't realize it was your birthday, Claire—Dave

just told me. Twenty-one ... it's a wonderful age to be, a turning point, sometimes, in a person's life. I wish you all the happiness in the world. Now, please allow an old woman to give you a little advice. Suffering is not an obstacle to happiness, but despair is. No matter what the future might have in store for you, never, never give in to despair. Everyone has a lucky star: the secret is, to believe in yours."

Aunt Suzanne went over to the desk and took a jewel case out of the drawer.

"This is only a little thing, but it's quite rare. It was made specially by an Italian jeweler. Give me your hand."

She wrapped a delicate, intricate bracelet around Claire's wrist.

"The wrist that once wore this was as small and lovely as yours," Aunt Suzanne said, in a voice that shook with emotion.

Claire realized that the memories attached to the bracelet were what gave it value—made it, indeed, priceless. She remembered Peter telling her about Aunt Suzanne's daughter who had died when she had been about Claire's age. She lifted her eyes to Aunt Suzanne's face, and saw the warmth and affection reflected in it.

Claire's response was immediate. The tenderness she had been keeping inside burst through the barriers of inhibition. She threw herself into the old woman's arms and kissed her. For a few moments, Aunt Suzanne held Claire close, understanding that, while the two of them were unalike in so many ways, each had a need that might find a response in the other. Inside Claire lived a little girl who was starved of love.

Inside Aunt Suzanne was a mother's love, in a heart desperately lonely for a daughter whom death had taken away.

CLAUDETTE RAMON QUICKLY DEMONSTRATED the quiet calm she had to offer as protection for Simon. Fairly large, and just over thirty, she was a woman who had decided long ago that nature had not been generous in endowing her with the kind of beauty and charm that were seen by so many to be necessary for a woman to be considered "feminine." She used no makeup, and kept her dark hair cut short and combed straight back.

Her constant contact with people who were ill had helped her to acquire an amiable philosophy, and she was rarely seen without a smile. Accustomed to consoling people, she brought comfort by always looking on the bright side of everything. No task seemed too much for her, no person too difficult to handle. She had discovered early in her career that the way to get on with people entrusted to her care was to learn to understand them.

During the day, she explained her theories to Claire.

With interest, Claire waited for dinner, hoping against hope that Miss Ramon's principles would be effective in their application to Simon's obstinate refusal to eat.

Finally, it became clear that this was to be one of the rare occasions when Claudette would have to admit defeat. She had never come across a mouth so tightly closed. Dinner lasted as long as it had the night before, eventually ending with Simon's acceptance of the usual glass of orange juice.

They were to leave the following morning at nine o'clock, and arrive in Brest the same evening. After a night at a hotel, Claire and Aunt Suzanne would board the ship, while Peter, Simon and Claudette took the plane. Aunt Suzanne had explained to Claire, somewhat shamefacedly, about her fear of airplanes, and Claire had firmly decided that she would accompany her. Claire would face that great expanse of water and come to terms with her phobia. Her decision made, she felt better immediately. She *would* do it, the devil *would* be exorcised.

Chapter 16

When Aunt Suzanne and Claire boarded the ship, Claire took a deep breath, and concentrating hard on the memory of Dave saying, "You can do it," she crossed the deck and looked down.

A momentary panic engulfed her as she stared, almost mesmerized, at the water, stretching almost as far as the eye could see. Still repeating under her breath, "You can do it, you can do it," she found that, in fact, she couldn't tear her eyes away.

Little by little, she became aware that a feeling of calm was descending on her, and that she was beginning to relax. There was still a strange unease, and a queasiness, but the pull of the water did not have anything like the effect on her it used to. She could cure herself, she knew it!

Giving a great sigh of relief, she turned away from the rail, a smile on her face.

The crossing was very smooth, and as a consequence Claire and Aunt Suzanne were able to spend most of the trip on deck in the fresh air. They were due to arrive at the island around noon. Simon, Peter and Claudette would be there well ahead of time and Aunt Suzanne had said that she knew she could count on Claudette to organize everything in the house. Claudette was a lady of many talents, thought Claire, while they were chatting about the nurse. Aunt Suzanne didn't have a thing to worry about in that direction.

Claire felt a combination of joie de vivre, peace and serenity, as she sat on the deck of the point contemplating the horizon. Life was good: love, security, warmth, a welcome home, a job . . . . Claire threw back her head and laughed—loudly, joyously. The first time she'd laughed in . . . how long?

PETER WAS WAITING FOR THEM on the dock. Simon hadn't come with him, he explained, because he was tired and had been put to bed.

They climbed the rugged path leading to the village, which consisted of a single, narrow street, lined on both sides with stone houses. Aunt Suzanne asked how anyone could ever maneuver a car in such confines.

"There are no cars on the island," said Peter, laughing. "At the very most, all you'll find are a few horse-drawn buggies, and the noise from them certainly won't keep you awake!"

As they walked down the street, they noticed a few small shops. Aunt Suzanne, looking worried, confided to Claire that she was glad they had arranged for cases of food and other provisions to be shipped ahead from the mainland.

As they continued to walk the houses became farther apart, surrounded by slightly larger gardens.

An easterly wind was cold and biting, and despite the brightness of the sun, they were shivering, as they walked, bent against the wind. Several small children ran to hide behind the low stone walls that surrounded the houses as the travelers walked by. The only other people on the street were a group of three women, their black skirts billowing in the wind, their dresses tied securely to their heads with broad ribbons.

"How dreary!" said Aunt Suzanne, looking tired and numb with the cold. "Not a tree in sight, and all the women seem to be in mourning!"

Claire was thinking that she couldn't feel any farther away from Dave if she had gone to another continent.

"Here we are!" announced Peter at last. "Welcome to Ty Breiz."

Confronting them was a house built low to the ground—presumably to withstand the onslaught of the incessant wind. The only thing that could be seen above the granite wall surrounding the well-kept property was the gable. The slate roof was very much in contrast to the roofs of the other houses, which were covered with stones or old tiles. However, this indication of luxury seemed to do little to impress Aunt Suzanne.

"It's so small and depressing!" she said to Peter.

Without answering, he opened the gate and stepped aside, letting the two women precede him onto the property.

They both let out a cry of pleasure.

Protected from the elements by the two wings of the house was an exquisite garden. Bright red geraniums were everywhere, as well as wallflowers in hues ranging from white to deepest purple. There was a profusion of tulips and irises, multicolored and beautiful. The paths were lined with dwarf palm trees, and carefully trimmed trees formed a haven of green in the center of it all. The walls of the house itself were covered in ivy.

"What a beautiful place!" whispered Claire, awe-struck.

Then they all went into the house, and Peter gave them a tour of the inside. In one wing was the large living room and kitchen and in the other wing were three bedrooms and a bathroom. Unfortunately, the house had been designed with summer living in mind. All the fireplaces were in use, but not much heat was coming out in the rooms. And the water in the bathroom was cold, without any means, apparently, for heating it.

"Tell me, Peter," asked Aunt Suzanne after she and Claire had made a full inspection, "how is the place lit at night?"

"Oil lamps or candles, whichever you prefer," he said. "I've brought along several flashlights to put in the bedrooms. Consider yourselves lucky to have a telephone, and water in the reservoir on the roof behind the house. Luckily, it rained a lot last winter."

Claudette Ramon had already unpacked most of the cases and almost everything had been put in place. Two local women were busy in the kitchen, and enticing smells wafted through the house.

"Where's Simon?" asked Claire. "I haven't seen him anywhere."

"In one of the gables," answered Peter. "He claimed it the moment he saw it. He can see the ocean and the lighthouse from his window. I think he's going to enjoy it here. Well, Claire, what do you think of the place?"

"I think it's wonderful, and the fact that Simon seems to have settled down already—enough to be resting—is a good omen!"

"Yes, well," sighed Aunt Suzanne, "perhaps it's just because I'm getting old, or I'm tired, but at the moment, all I can see are the drawbacks. Oh, well, no doubt I'll get used to it, and as you say, if Simon likes it, that's the main thing!"

BUT AS THE DAYS WENT BY, the little boy's health showed no signs of improvement. After two weeks on the island, he still had the same pallor and it was still a daily struggle to get him to eat anything.

Before leaving the island, Peter had insisted that Simon stay within the sheltered area of the garden for a time, in order that he acclimatize gradually to the rugged island weather.

Lying on a lawn chair in the garden one day, Simon listened drowsily as Claire told him more of the adventures of King Arthur and his brave knights.

Suddenly, his eyes opened wide. "I see something!" he whispered.

Something had moved on the wall, behind the climbers clinging to the stone. The two of them kept staring at the spot, but could only see the shadow of the leaves on the stones.

Then Claire saw a branch move. Simon got up and walked toward the wall.

A head of shaggy, sun-bleached hair gradually appeared over the wall. It was a boy with a freckled face. Eyes the color of the ocean stared at Simon, then at Claire, with unabashed curiosity.

"What's your name?" asked Simon.

"Tugdual. What's yours?"

"What a funny name! Where did you get it? Mine's Simon."

"Aren't you allowed to go out? It's my grandfather's name—he said lots of boys had that name when he was little."

"No, I can't go out of the garden, it's too windy."

"If you have to wait till the wind stops, you're never going to get out of the garden!"

"Claire, can he come in?" asked Simon, turning to Claire his eyes alight with excitement.

"I don't see why not," said Claire. "Jump down carefully, Tugdual."

The boy quickly scrambled over the wall and jumped down next to Simon. He looked about seven or eight. His tanned face and sturdy body contrasted sharply with Simon's pallor and frailty.

They looked at each other for a while.

"Did you come over by boat?" asked Tugdual.

Simon proudly stuck out his chest. "Not me. I came by plane. Have you ever been in a plane?"

"Not yet. But I will some day," shot back the other boy defensively. "And I'm going to drive in a car and ride on a train, too!"

"It's more fun on a plane. Everybody likes to go in a plane."

"I've never even seen a real car," confessed Tugdual, suddenly shy.

Simon couldn't think of a thing to say. It was obviously beyond his comprehension. "Wait a minute," he said, and disappeared into the house. When he came back out, Claire saw that he was carrying a shoe box. Putting it on the ground, he opened the lid, disclosing his precious collection of miniature cars.

He handed three cars to the dazzled Tugdual.

"These are for you," he said. "Now, let's play with the rest of them."

"No," said Tugdual, stuffing the cars into his pocket. "You come to my house, so I can give you something, too."

Simon turned back once more to Claire, his little face pleading. "Oh, may we, Claire? Oh, please say yes!"

Claire had been very touched and pleased with Simon's generosity to the stranger. Looking up at the sky, which was quite clear, she agreed. "I don't see much harm in it. Let's all go!"

Outside of the protection of the walls, the wind took their breaths away. Claire took one of Simon's hands, and Tugdual said gently, "Here, Simon, take my hand, too. It's just because you're not used to it."

Practically holding each other up, the three managed to keep going until they reached a white stucco house standing alone on a sandy spit.

An old man sat in front of the house, smoking his pipe.

"Grandpa!" shouted Tugdual. "I've brought Simon—see what he gave me! Oh, and Miss . . . er . . . ."

"Claire de Montebourg," said Claire, holding out her hand to the old man. "I hope we're not intruding!"

"Not in the least," said the old man, getting up from his stool and taking her hand in his gnarled, tanned fingers. "And this is Simon, eh? Lord, he's a skinny one! Maryvonne! Come see!" he called into the house.

A young woman dressed in black came to the door. The look on her face indicated to Claire that she, too, was taken aback by Simon's thinness. But she simply said, "Hello! Please come in."

Inside, Claire and Simon looked around them in wonder. It was the simple interior of a fisherman's cottage, but on shelves, tables, hanging from the walls and ceilings, in every nook and cranny, were boats of all shapes and sizes, meticulously handcarved. They had masts and tiny sails that shivered in the breeze, like the wings of a butterfly.

Awestruck, Simon was wide-eyed and speechless as he looked around his new friend's house.

"My grandfather made them all," explained Tugdual, not without pride. "His legs were hurt and he couldn't fish anymore, so he carved all these boats, just with a knife!"

Simon turned to look at the old man, who was walking toward the fireplace, clearing his throat, to spit into the fire. The boy was beside himself with admiration.

"Seeing as how you're a friend of Tugdual's," said the old man, "and if Miss de Montebourg will permit, I think I'll give you a boat. Here . . . here's a two-master. Would you like to have this one?"

Carefully, he put a small ship in the palm of Simon's hand. It was complete with sails and rigging. Simon was mute with joy.

"That's really very generous of you. Are you sure about giving it away?" Claire asked the old man.

He looked at her intently, and then at the small boy, bent lovingly over his present. "Yes, I meant it. I know he'll look after it, and as you can see, I've got plenty!" He smiled warmly at Claire, revealing two or three missing teeth.

"Well, Simon," said Claire, "we must be going now. Say . . . ."

"Oh, thank you very much!" said Simon breathlessly. "I've never had a ship like this, and I'll keep it safe, I promise you!"

"You can come back any time and play with Tugdual," said the boy's mother. "And I hope you'll be able to come, too, Miss de Montebourg."

Repeating their thanks, Claire and Simon went out of the house and turned toward their own house, Simon sheltering the precious ship under his jacket.

The next morning, when Simon came down to breakfast, Claire looked at him and her heart lifted. He really did look a bit better, and there was definitely some color in his cheeks. She looked at Claudette, who had come down with Simon, who was smiling happily.

"And who slept all night with his ship?" Claudette asked Simon, teasingly. "Now you must eat your breakfast, so you can be strong enough to go and visit Tugdual and his family again soon!"

And to the adults' amazement, Simon actually started to eat.

Claire took Claudette aside, and whispered to her, "He looks so much better this morning, I can hardly believe it. Do you think that possibly we could try doing without his injections for a day or two? You know how he hates them."

"I was just thinking exactly the same thing," agreed Claudette. "He seems so happy this morning, and that'll do him far more good than any medication."

They both looked back at Simon, sitting at the table, contentedly munching on a newly baked biscuit, smothered in honey, his model ship sitting beside his plate.

Chapter 17

When the time came for his lesson the next day, Simon showed up immediately, looking suspiciously angelic, and sat down in front of his textbooks. Claire looked questioningly at him. Normally, he had to be almost dragged into the room and more than once had to be found where he had hidden himself in some new secret spot.

Simon's feigning studiousness was not successful and there was a flicker of mischief in his eyes that was not missed by Claire. She also noticed that he had put on his shoes, instead of wearing the slippers he normally wore, with the thick lining as insulation against the cold stone floors. Claire said nothing, but made a mental note to stay on her guard.

"I . . . . May I get my storybook? I forgot it."

"Where is it?" asked Claire.

"I left it in the garden."

Claire agreed. There was no risk in that. The gate had been locked.

When she went out to call him, a few minutes later,

he had disappeared. Annoyed, she went back indoors and met Claudette in the hall.

"I saw Simon climbing the wall from my window," the nurse said. "Don't worry, I think it does him good to run on the moors. Yesterday, for the first time in ages, he ate everything that was put in front of him. Mind you, next time I think we'll leave the gate open. It might be a lot safer!"

That afternoon, Simon and Claire went for a walk on the moors. Nothing much had been said about the morning's escapade, for which Simon appeared very grateful.

They wandered over the moor, picking little blue and yellow flowers and Simon gathered beautiful shells, where they had been carried onto the grass by the sea wind. They had only been walking for about five minutes, when they spied a small figure in the distance, clambering among the rocks.

"It's Tugdual!" shouted Simon, running toward the distant figure.

And Tugdual indeed it turned out to be, as Claire discovered on nearing the two boys.

"Good afternoon, Miss de Montebourg," said Tugdual politely. "Simon says you're out for a walk. May I come along with you?"

"Well, of course. We'd be delighted to have you along, and you can show us the sights!" Claire smiled as she looked down at the two upturned, shining faces.

The three of them spent a wonderful afternoon, petting some funny-looking black sheep tied in pairs to stakes in order to graze, and wandering far and wide across the wind-swept moors. When Simon looked a little tired, Claire suggested that they sit down, in the shelter of a stone wall. Simon produced two miniature cars from his pocket, and he and Tugdual played races with them.

It was late in the afternoon by the time they got back to Tugdual's house. Maryvonne, Tugdual's mother, was cooking dinner and the appetizing smell of cabbage soup filled the house.

Hungry from the fresh sea air, Claire thought that she had never smelled anything as good as that in her whole life, and, judging from Simon's expression, he hadn't either. He shyly asked what the good smell was, and Maryvonne lifted the lid from the pot hanging over the fire on a spit in the fireplace. "Would you like to try some?" she asked.

"Oh, yes! Could I?" asked Simon, delighted.

With a smile, Maryvonne placed steaming, aromatic bowls in front of Tugdual and the two guests.

After they'd finished, Claire and Simon thanked Maryvonne, and linking hands, they walked contentedly back to Ty Breitz through the windy darkness.

Claire had been afraid that Simon would be overtired from all his exertions that day, but when they arrived home, to be met by a smiling Aunt Suzanne, Simon climbed the stairs without a single protest, and fell asleep almost as soon as his tousled head hit the pillow.

ON A CLEAR BRIGHT DAY about three weeks later Dr. Breveley was expected, and Claire went to meet him at the small airstrip. She was surprised when Peter alighted from the plane. He explained to her that his father had been called away to perform a very delicate emergency operation in Italy, and so he had come instead.

In a friendly gesture, Peter slipped his arm around Claire's shoulders as they walked back to Ty Breitz. Claire liked Peter very much and was happy to be able to spend a day with him. She felt at ease in his presence, and found his company amusing.

But she couldn't wait any more than a few minutes before asking the question that had been burning her lips. "Peter . . . I meant to ask you . . . have you seen Dave?"

"Dave who?" he asked, laughing at her teasingly. "Good heavens, you don't wait to give me a minute to enjoy my illusions! As a matter of fact, I saw him yesterday."

He didn't say another word, but just kept smiling at her, his eyes flashing with mischief.

"How is he?" asked Claire in a voice that trembled a little, despite her efforts to keep it casual.

"He's fine. Working too hard, of course . . . as usual." He looked at Claire out of the corner of his eye and then continued. "He gave me a letter for you."

She blushed self-consciously as she took the letter. Her first letter from Dave. . . . She decided to wait until she was back in her room at Ty Breitz alone, before reading it, so she could fully enjoy it.

PETER WAS SURPRISED AND DELIGHTED to see the change in his little brother. The change had been less noticeable to Aunt Suzanne and the rest of the household, since they had been with Simon day by day. But Peter was immensely pleased with the boy's progress, and thoroughly approved of Claire's and Claudette's decision to discontinue the shots.

At lunch, Peter was amazed to see Simon eat the entire meal placed in front of him.

After the meal, Maria, the local girl they had hired as a maid, brought in the coffee, and Claire could see immediately that something was wrong. Maria was biting her lips and looking very upset.

"What is it, Maria?" she asked. "Is something wrong?"

"It's not me! It's the little boy. . . ."

Four heads turned in the direction of Simon, who was calmly eating his dessert.

"What's he done?" asked Aunt Suzanne.

"Oh, he hasn't done anything, the poor little thing!" came the answer.

Deciding not to ask any more questions, Aunt Suzanne waited patiently for the woman to give them some sort of explanation.

"He's been playing with Tugdual, hasn't he?" Maria went on. "Do you know why the boy hasn't been at school?"

All eyes were fixed on the maid. The room was silent.

"He's got the measles, that's why," she said finally. "I saw his mother yesterday and she told me Tugdual's in his bed, as red as a beet! So you see *madame*, there's a good chance that Simon will soon have the measles, too!"

On those words, she turned and walked out of the room back to the kitchen.

SIMON, IN FACT, DID NOT fall victim to the measles, but for the next three weeks, he spent all his time playing on the moors alone. His cheeks were rounding out, and his little bones no longer stuck out so pitifully from his skin.

To compensate for Tugdual's absence Aunt Su-

zanne, Claire and Claudette took turns taking Simon
to a sheltered part of the beach to play. Other times
they would walk for hours over the island. Sometimes
they would sit outside Tugdual's house, listening to
his grandfather telling stories. They loved to listen to
the local legends, which he embellished with details
from his own, vivid imagination, and told with great
conviction.

The stories had a strange effect on Claire. Each time,
she would come away feeling twinges of melancholy
and renewed anxiety. Feelings that were, however,
instantly relieved whenever there was a letter from
Dave. Her imagination would exaggerate every word,
and her heart would feel a burst of happiness.
Perhaps, after all this time, there was still hope. But
when more than two weeks would go by without
word from him, she would again find herself on the
brink of depression. At such times, when she felt the
small dark cloud descending on her, she would seek
out Claudette and talk to her. Usually, this worked
effectively to lift her spirits, at least for a time.

IT WAS JUNE NOW, and no one would have recognized
the beautiful little boy as the Simon of Milhouse. He
was tanned a golden brown and had gained just
enough weight to give his body healthy, sturdy pro-
portions. Now he looked much the same as the other
little boys on the island. Dave had been right about the
sea air, and Aunt Suzanne kept saying so, over and
over again.

But the transformation had been accompanied by a
vitality that had become nothing short of devastating.
Quite often, Simon would find ways to use his energy
that would create havoc all around him.

Some days, he would come home bruised and scratched, with his clothes badly torn. Tugdual and Simon would join the other boys, and the way he looked when he got home spoke eloquently of the rough-and-tumble games Simon had been playing with his friends.

The army of young boys seemed to grow larger every day, and their war cries would often resound around Ty Breitz. It was then that Aunt Suzanne put her foot down, one day preventing Simon from joining them.

"Please, let me play with them! Please, Aunt Suzanne! Just for a little while."

"No, Simon, not this time. There are too many of them. You're going to rest, for a change."

"But I don't want to rest," the boy cried, his eyes filling with tears.

"But, Simon, if you go out there, you'll just get beaten up again!"

"So what?" Simon answered, his face crimson. "We have lots of fun together. . . ."

Claudette put an end to a discussion that seemed as though it might go in circles forever. From her window, she had just seen a flotilla of ships with red sails approaching the island. It was a spectacle not to be missed. Simon agreed, and followed the nurse.

Aunt Suzanne took advantage of the respite and went into the village to do some shopping. Claire had decided to explore the northern coast of the island, which she had not yet seen. When she had Simon with her, it had been necessary to go to the bays on the south shore, where there was more shelter.

A few days earlier, she had received another letter from Dave, telling her that he would be coming to the

island some time in June. Even though he had not
given her a definite date, it was enough for Claire just
to know that she would be seeing him again soon. She
wondered how she'd managed to survive this long so
far away from him. Then again, when she stopped to
think about it, her stay on the island had been really
enjoyable. She loved Simon, had become very close to
Aunt Suzanne, and learned the meaning of real
friendship with Claudette.

She followed the path across the middle of the
island. She had never felt any particular urge to go in
this direction—in fact, she had been a little apprehensive about it, probably because of the ruins that could
be seen at the top of the hill. There was something
sinister about the look of them. She felt an involuntary
shudder as she started to walk around them.

To one side of the ruins, she saw a strongly con-
structed building with a concrete road leading from it
to the moors.

That's strange, she thought to herself. *Why would
anyone build a garage on an island where there are no cars?
And such a large one, too. . . .*

The path began to climb upward, and when Claire
reached the top, she saw the white lighthouse whose
beam swept across the back of Ty Breitz at night. She
was walking quickly, pushed from behind by a strong
wind out of the southwest. A storm wind, the old fishermen called it. Their accuracy in predicting the weather had become a source of wonderment to them all.

She reached the tip of the island. There were no
jagged outcrops here, as were common elsewhere,
just the barren bluffs that fell steeply into the sea,
some ninety feet down. The top of the cliffs was
shrouded in mist.

Claire tried to step back, only to find that she couldn't move. Neither could she see the waves or the lighthouse. The ground seemed to be shifting beneath her feet, and a black wall was inexorably rising in front of her eyes. The dizziness . . . it was coming back to torture her, tearing at her insides, crushing her will. In a supreme effort, she dug her nails into the palms of her hands, but she had lost all sense of equilibrium. She fell like a dead bird to the ground, clutching desperately at a small clump of windswept grass with her shaking hands.

Fortunately, she had fallen some distance back from the edge of the cliff. On hands and knees, sobbing desperately, she dragged herself to safety—some sixty feet—to a hollow from which she could see nothing but the solid ground under her and the sky above.

Suddenly, she was filled with disgust at herself. Why had she crawled to safety instead of walking? To avoid answering the call to suicide buried deep in her mind? The marvels of medical science might be able to detect the slightest sign of actual damage to the brain, but only when the problem was physical. Nothing, it seemed, could probe effectively when the problem was connected with the thought process. This was where the evil lay, an evil as destructive to the mind as cancer cells to the body. And, apparently, with the cure equally elusive. She really thought that she'd managed to cure herself through sheer willpower. But, by concentrating on her new job, she had achieved the destruction of only one thing: her self-absorption. The rest of it had remained the same, dormant for a time, but impossible to dominate. The hereditary illness would always be there, lurking in the background, waiting to show itself each time she began to feel despair or any kind of anxiety. She thought of Dave and felt such pain that she buried her face in her hands and wept.

IT WAS THIS WAY that Aunt Suzanne found her. Feeling worried by Claire's prolonged absence, Aunt Suzanne had set out to look for her. She sat down next to Claire and with gentle hands took Claire's head onto her lap.

"What is it, dear?" she asked tenderly. "Tell me, aren't you happy here with us? I should have known, you must be very lonely.... That's it, isn't it?"

"Oh, no ... you've been so kind! It's just me ... being silly...."

"That's not it? Then ...."

She stopped and looked intently at Claire. "My dear, tell me ... is it Dave?"

Deciding that it would be better if Aunt Suzanne didn't know the truth, Claire agreed that it was Dave.

"But what's the problem, Claire, my dear? He'll be here very soon. You're young and beautiful, and certainly one of the most openhearted and generous people I've ever met. You have everything you need to be happy! Just concentrate on the good things, on your blessings, instead of harboring the black thoughts!"

Aunt Suzanne's words were very comforting. "Openhearted and generous" she had said. It was the one compliment that could move Claire. It proved to her that, by exercising her will, she had at least accomplished something.

Shakily, Claire got to her feet, putting out a hand to help Aunt Suzanne. They hugged each other.

"My dear," said Aunt Suzanne, "you're going to be very happy, you'll see, and I'm going to do everything in my power to help. Now, I have something to show you. I just got a letter from Marie, at Milhouse. Apparently a man has been to the house, twice, to see you. Marie completely forgot about it, which is why she hadn't mentioned it before. The man came back last week and seemed very annoyed about not being able to get in touch with you. Poor Marie must be getting old—she says that she's enclosing the gentleman's card, but it isn't in the envelope. She must have forgotten to put it in.''

''Did Marie tell him where I was?''

''No. I'll write and ask her to send on the man's card, but it'll be another four or five days before the next mail leaves the island.''

Claire wondered who the man could have been. Her father? She wished that Marie had remembered to put the card into her letter. Oliver? It couldn't have been Oliver, she decided; the break with him had been final and besides, neither man knew where she was. Then who would have come to Milhouse to see her?

Aunt Suzanne broke into her thoughts, hesitantly. ''I know, through Dave, that you left your family because you were very unhappy at home. I'm only bringing this up because of the affection I feel for you. There's something that's been bothering me. Youth sometimes can be very cruel when it acts irrationally, never knowing what grief may have been left in its wake. Do you think you could possible make another effort to reconcile yourself with your father? At least promise me that you'll think about it!''

Claire promised that she would, and holding onto each other, the two women managed to get back to the house, struggling against the ever increasing wind.

Chapter 18

Soon after midnight, Claire was awakened by a loud crash. As the brief flash of light shone from the lighthouse into her room, she could see what had happened. Despite the fastened shutters, the wind had blown the window open and everything had been knocked off the dresser by the flying curtains.

She jumped out of bed and ran to the window, pushing against it with all her strength to close it against the force of the wind.

This must be nearly a hurricane, she thought. *It sounds as if the whole house is going to cave in.*

The sound of the wind through the cracks in the shutters was a long, continuous howl.

Suddenly, Claire remembered there were no shutters on Simon's windows. Quickly donning a housecoat, she grabbed her flashlight and hurried out into the hallway.

When she reached the door to Aunt Suzanne's room, she stopped to listen for a moment. There was nothing to be heard but the harsh howling of the wind.

When she reached the gable, she found Aunt Suzanne and Claudette struggling to cover the window with a blanket.

"It's blowing as hard here as it will be on the beach," said the nurse.

Although the window was still closed, the blanket was billowing like the mainsail of a great ship, and the room was filled with the sound of creaking.

Once the drafts seemed to have been effectively eliminated, Aunt Suzanne suggested that they go back to bed. Simon was sound asleep. The wind ruffled his hair, but didn't disturb him.

In the morning, the storm still lashed the island with unabated fury. Heavy rain had turned the street into a river, raging through the middle of the village. In the fields, it was washing away the meager crops and topsoil.

The relatively sheltered garden of Ty Breitz looked like a disaster area, with all the flowers mutilated and broken.

The two women from the island were late getting to work, and all morning the conversation revolved around past disasters that had struck the island, and the amount of damage that the present one was wreaking. No boats had been over from the mainland for a couple of days because of high seas. Consequently, no one on the island had received mail or newspapers.

Claire tried hard to keep Simon occupied, but it was an uphill struggle. He seemed petulant and easily bored and wouldn't settle to anything for any length of time. It was with relief, therefore, that in the early afternoon when the wind died down markedly, Claire spotted Tugdual struggling up to their door, completely swathed in outsized raingear.

Simon and Tugdual racketted round the house all day, making the walls reverberate with their war cries and shouts. Everyone's tempers were a little short, and the living room was strewn with what looked like every single one of Simon's toys.

Claudette, whose patience seemed without limit, decided to send Tugdual back home and to put Simon to bed an hour earlier than usual.

It was like the old days, back at Milhouse. No matter how much he was coaxed, Simon refused to eat his food.

"I'm not surprised that he won't eat," commented Aunt Suzanne. "Being cooped up in the house all day; I'll be glad when he can go back outside to play."

Claire said nothing, but she didn't like the way the boy looked. She didn't want to worry the others, and it was possible that the flush on his cheeks was the result of all those strenuous games with Tugdual. But she noticed that Claudette, also, was giving the boy sidelong glances and frowning a little. Claire volunteered to help Claudette put Simon to bed, and then she realized he was shivering.

"Claudette, do you think he's got a fever?" Claire asked anxiously.

"He may have; I'll just get out the thermometer and check. He's certainly very warm to the touch."

When she withdrew the thermometer from Simon's uncomplaining mouth, her eyebrows rose in consternation. "It's really quite high. You'd better fetch Mrs. Chanoy."

Claire ran to fetch Aunt Suzanne, who leaned over the boy and felt his burning forehead.

"Perhaps he's caught a chill from playing in the drafty house," she said with concern. "I'll go and get him some bouillon."

But Simon refused to touch even a mouthful of the soup.

"We must call the doctor, right away!" said Aunt Suzanne and ran downstairs to the telephone. But the line was dead; they were isolated from the rest of the island . . . cut off from the rest of the world.

Claire and Aunt Suzanne sat in the living room, trying to console each other. They told each other that Simon was in good health, now, and much like any other healthy child, was running a high temperature because of a touch of the flu or some other minor ailment. In the morning, he'd be as good as new.

But neither of them believed what they were saying, and soon Claire got up, offering to go down to the village and find the doctor. She wrapped herself up in two sweaters and a raincoat and started out.

The angry force of the wind that had risen again, fought her every step of the way. She had to wait for the beacon from the lighthouse to light her way. She crouched down as she walked, making herself as small as she could, offering as little resistance as possible to the wind. After many stops, she finally reached the doctor's house, and a maid answered the door.

Claire had to shout to be heard.

"The doctor isn't here," the woman shouted back. "He had to go to Brest, on the mainland, and hasn't been able to get back because of the storm. I hope it's not too serious?"

"I hope so, too," said Claire fervently. "Thank you, anyway."

Her journey back to the house was equally hazardous, but this time the wind was at her back, and staying on her feet was a major problem. Almost helpless against the thrust of the wind, she literally ran most of the way home.

She found Aunt Suzanne and Claudette in Simon's room, bent over the little boy, and told them the bad news about the doctor. Simon couldn't sleep and was tossing and turning, unable to tell them where it hurt. Then he hurriedly got out of bed, bent over in pain, and was sick. Claire did what she could to help the nurse.

Simon was as white as the sheets when he climbed back into bed. He closed his eyes, and they hoped he would go off to sleep, but a few minutes later he was curled up in a ball again, crying with pain.

Claudette pulled back the sheet, loosened the boy's pajamas and put her hand on his burning abdomen. Simon screamed.

"Oh, my heavens!" said Claudette. "It looks like appendicitis."

"What on earth are we going to do?" cried Aunt Suzanne in distress.

There was no refrigeration at Ty Breitz, but the tap water was ice cold. Claire, under Claudette's instructions, made primitive cold compresses by soaking towels in the cold water. They were better than nothing, although not much help. They had to be changed every few minutes, because, once placed on Simon's fiery stomach, they heated up quickly.

However, the treatment seemed to offer a little relief

to the child and finally he fell asleep, albeit a fitful one, broken often by a sigh or a moan.

Claire insisted that Aunt Suzanne go to bed. She promised that she and Claudette would stay at the boy's bedside, and finally the older woman agreed.

The moment Aunt Suzanne had left the room, the two young women expressed their fears.

"What's going to happen, Claudette? I'm scared."

"Let's try to keep calm," the nurse replied. "But I think we'd better start praying that this storm lets up soon."

A few hours later, Simon was awake again, sitting up in bed, screaming, tears pouring down his face. The cold compresses had to be applied again.

"I don't know what we're going to do if the pain gets any worse," whispered Claudette to Claire. "If only the doctor had been here, he could have operated."

Claire was so preoccupied looking after Simon that she hadn't noticed the change in the weather outside. The storm had departed as quickly as it had arrived.

"Oh, Claire, help me a moment, would you . . . ?"

Simon was being sick again, his face contorted in pain. Then he lost consciousness.

Aunt Suzanne had come in to relieve Claire. She saw the inert body of the boy in Claudette's arms and staggered suddenly. Claire quickly got up and went to her, helping her into a chair.

"We can't let this happen," said Aunt Suzanne in a faint, trembling voice. "Claire, Claudette . . . there must be something we can do!"

While Claire sat on the arm of Aunt Suzanne's chair, one arm around Aunt Suzanne to comfort her, Claudette sponged Simon's forehead. Finally a little color appeared and he opened his eyes. "Oh, it hurts! It hurts so much!"

Aunt Suzanne took the child in her arms and held him close, murmuring comforting, loving words.

"Let me try and examine him again, Mrs. Chanoy," said Claudette. She finally managed to straighten Simon's legs enough to examine his abdomen. Claire held his legs while Claudette gently probed with her hand. "He'll have to be operated on right away," Claudette said. "Now that the wind has died down, there must be some way we can get him to the mainland."

Just at that moment, a long, low, eerie sound reached their ears. The fog horn! There would be no way now for them to leave the island by sea. Looking out of the window, Claire couldn't see even as far as the garden. Aunt Suzanne was crying softly, as she held the little boy in her arms.

"If only this island was populated with someone else besides fishermen!" muttered Claudette.

"Yes, the doctor," murmured Aunt Suzanne. "But what's the use of thinking of that, now?"

"I wasn't thinking about the doctor. What we need is a pilot. There's a plane here. The first time I came to the island with Dr. Breveley, the owner's son came over to join us in his private plane. We all went back to Orly airport together, so that means his plane is still here. But the men on this island know how to handle boats, not planes!"

"Where is this plane?" asked Claire.

"In the hangar, near the old ruins."

Claire remembered the new building she had thought was a large garage when she had seen it on her walk to the north shore. She looked back at Simon.

He was pale and his golden curls were sticking to his forehead with perspiration. It was quite clear to all of them in the room that time was running out.

Claire drew a deep, shaky breath. "I have a pilot's license," she lied in an unrecognizable voice. "I can fly that plane."

Having said it, her mind raced in a panic. How would she remember all the things that Oliver had taught her? He'd told her that she had the makings of a natural pilot, but she hadn't progressed that far before that awful time when the vertigo had overcome her, and after that she'd never flown again. Taking off would be simple enough, as long as the plane was roughly similar to the one that she'd been used to, but landing? Well, she'd have to worry about landing when the time came. This was their one and only chance to save Simon, and she had to do it.

"Claire!" Aunt Suzanne was weeping as she hugged the young girl. "We must leave right away. I'll try and get messages through to Brest airport and to the hospital—if the telephone lines are back up, that is. Hurry, a few minutes might mean the difference between life and death!"

"Are you sure you won't get lost over the ocean, in this fog?" asked Claudette, staring at Claire with wide, frightened eyes.

"Don't worry," said Claire with a conviction in her voice that was totally false. "I can fly by instruments. Once the compass is set, the rest is easy."

She rushed out of the room, and came back with a map of the area, which she and the other two women went over hastily. By setting a course due east, she'd be able to follow the coastline, then head for Brest, which should be visible from the air.

"Wrap up Simon warmly, Mrs. Chanoy," instructed Claudette. "I'll run to the lighthouse to see if someone can send those messages. Claire, you'd better change into dry clothes, or you'll freeze in the plane."

Claire ran to her room and threw on some dry, warm clothes. Then, running out of the house, she made her way up to the hangar, knocking frantically on doors on her way, to get some of the men to help carry Simon and get the plane out of the hangar.

Claire was able to enlist the help of three men. The problem was for them to get from the main street of the village to the hangar at the north end of the island in the thick of the fog. It was solid, like a gray shroud covering everything, including themselves. None of them could see ten feet in any direction; only the locals' familiarity with the island's geography prevented them from walking around in circles. At length their unerring instinct brought them to their destination. The going had been slow, and Claire's nerves screamed with tension.

More time was lost as they tugged at the hangar doors. After several frantic tries, they managed to get the doors open. Claire looked over the controls while Aunt Suzanne got Simon into the plane.

The men had pulled the plane out when Claudette arrived, panting. "I can't get the messages through, right now, but I'll keep trying, Claire." She peered fearfully at the small plane. "Is there going to be enough fuel?"

"I . . . I'm not sure."

Claudette looked at Claire, realization slowly dawning on her face. She grabbed the younger woman's arm. "Claire, you lied. You don't have your. . . ."

"Listen to me," interrupted Claire in a fierce whisper. "It's our only chance to save Simon, you said so yourself. No, I don't have my license, but I do know how to fly a plane. The only thing I have to worry about is the landing . . . and with God's help, I'm pretty sure I can pull it off."

Claudette didn't answer, but her face showed clearly her apprehension.

Claire stepped into the cockpit and buckled herself in. With enormous relief, she saw that this plane was very like the one she had flown in before. Speaking out loud, she methodically went through the checklist. Then, with a final look back at Simon, lying behind her seat, she took a deep breath and prayed.

When she finally had a moment to take a breath, she was surprised to find that she had executed a near-perfect take-off, and that the little figures left on the ground, their white faces turned upward, were already almost lost in the mist.

Claire had the strange sensation of being suspended. She couldn't see a thing except the propeller beating through the dense fog. Not a sign of land or sky. Nothing to help her get a single bearing . . . . and it was beginning to get dark.

Oliver's instructions, buried deep in her mind, had helped her with the take-off, and she began to breathe more normally. She leaned forward to switch the radio on, but, to her consternation, she could hear nothing except the high-pitched, harsh crackle of static. There was so much electricity in the air that no communication, Claire knew, would be able to penetrate the interference.

Maybe, she thought, steadfastly quelling her rising fear, if she climbed a little higher, she might manage to get clear of the fog. She pulled back gently on the stick and felt the plane begin to climb. When she had reached a height where the fog was a little less dense, she levelled off. For the first time, Claire could see patches of sky, gray black in the twilight. But she still didn't have any idea of her position. All she knew was that she had taken off heading north, and that she'd have to make a turn to the east and head for the coast.

Gripping her trembling lower lip between her teeth, she gingerly started to turn the plane, only slightly reassured by how obedient the controls were.

She looked back to see how Simon was doing. He was very pale and his nostrils were pinched. Claire wiped away the tears that had come to her eyes and turned her attention resolutely to finding her bearings.

The fog was thinning. Suddenly she sighted land, and began to veer south to find Brest, keeping her eyes on the compass.

She reduced the fuel input and gently pushed the stick away from her. Shapes of houses and trees, fields and barns, quickly became discernible and grew steadily larger before her eyes. She felt a momentary panic, but managed to level off in time. She tasted blood in her mouth, and realized that she had bitten her lip hard. She could see, looking down, the people below looking up in alarm at the small plane almost brushing the tree tops.

Then suddenly, she saw something move out of the corner of her eye. She looked around, and saw a small plane similar to her own flying alongside. Then it picked up speed and flew out in front of her, and she realized what was happening.

It had come to guide her, to help her to make the necessary maneuvers. Claudette must have got at least one of the messages through! With a prayer of thanks, she followed the plane, which had started to climb.

The whole scene slowly took on an aura of complete unreality. In spite of the cold, Claire was aware that her body was bathed in perspiration.

The airport loomed up in the distance, and Claire had began to laugh with relief. "We're almost there, Simon," Claire said, half laughing, half crying. But she knew the words were for herself, as the little boy was unconscious behind her.

The plane ahead of her increased its speed, drawing away from her. She watched carefully while the plane ahead landed. She leaned forward, her eyes glued to the small plane, watching it drop down and then level off close to the ground before giving a slight bump, which showed it had landed.

She reached the point where her plane must start its descent. A sudden, indescribable terror overtook her. She'd never be able to do it. She couldn't move a muscle. She groped frantically in her mind, and seemed to hear a calm voice reciting the instructions for landing. That must be Oliver, she thought distractedly. But why did it sound like Dave's voice? Desperately, she fought to follow the instructions—how long had she been flying? It felt like several days.

Then, unbelievably, she felt a jarring shock under the wheels, then another and another. . . . The plane was veering hard to the right, she could feel it. She fought with all her strength, trying to keep the plane going straight ahead while she reached forward and turned off the fuel. Finally, there came a rending, tearing sound, and the plane ground to a halt, off the runway just a few feet away from a clump of trees.

Someone was opening the cockpit door . . . there was a deafening sound of sirens . . . she felt herself being lifted and violently hugged against a tweed jacket that she knew so well. The dreamlike state continued, but she managed to gasp out, "Simon! Oh, do hurry! He's going to die!"

But the back of the plane was empty, and Claire saw, through a haze, an ambulance already pulling away. People were rushing toward her from all sides. Talking gently, softly, comfortingly, Dave half-carried Claire to his waiting car and started off for the hospital.

"THERE WASN'T MUCH TIME TO SPARE," the surgeon said to Dave. "Another hour or so, and his appendix would have burst. Fortunately, the boy seems in perfect health otherwise, and he'll pull through just fine."

Tense and exhausted, Claire waited for Simon to be brought out of the recovery room back to his own room. She couldn't stop shaking, and her head felt numb. But she had to hang on till she was sure that the ordeal was really over.

Dave and Claire stood together at Simon's bedside, waiting for the boy to open his eyes. Now, their lives were bound together by a feeling much stronger than passion, and at that moment, they were closer to each other than they ever had been before.

A nurse approached the bed, just as Simon opened his eyes. Claire smiled at Simon, then turned to look up at Dave, smiling, but her vision blurred. . . . She could hear the noise of the propeller growing louder and louder . . . then, through the mists, a voice, "Claire, darling . . . ." Then a black curtain fell.

Chapter 19

For more than two days, Claire lay in a hospital bed, struggling with the intense fever to which she had succumbed. When she opened her eyes, on the morning of the third day, the first face she saw was Claudette's.

"Oh, Claire, how wonderful! You're awake! I must go and telephone Dave."

"No, Claudette, wait a minute," Claire said, her voice faint. "Tell me something—is Simon really all right? And why was Dave at the airport waiting for me? And...."

"One question at a time!" interrupted Claudette, laughing. "Yes, Simon's fine, and going back to Milhouse with Mrs. Chanoy in a couple of days. And Dave had to go back to his patients this morning—but up until last night, he's been sitting with you constantly; we couldn't even get him to rest! He called Dr. Breveley when you collapsed, and he dropped everything and came rushing over here—you've certainly had the best medical care available. Now, was that everything? Oh, no. Well, Dave happened to be in Brest when you landed there quite by chance. He'd apparently decided to take his vacation ten days earlier than he'd originally thought, and he planned to surprise you on the island, instead of which, he got a pretty nasty surprise himself. When the fog started to lift, he'd gone rushing to the airport, wanting to catch the first available plane over to the island, and the moment he got there, they broadcast over the PA system for a doctor, that there was going to be an emergency landing of a small plane from the island. Can you imagine how he felt when *you* fell out of the cockpit?''

Claire turned her thoughts to Simon and the news that he was making such good progress. Although she was very glad to know that he would soon be as good as new, could it mean that her role as his teacher had come to an end? She'd come to love his family very much.

And Dave . . . would she be separated from him, too? She remembered the face she loved so much, bending over her, recalling every detail with such accuracy that it brought a sharp pain to her heart. Words buzzed in her head: "Claire darling." Had Dave really said them, or had they just been wishful thinking, a product of her fevered imagination?

"Now," said Claudette, "I'll go and call Dave. He said he was going to come and get you, himself, as soon as you are well enough to travel."

To take me where, wondered Claire to herself. *I have no home anymore. . . .*

The next day, Dr. Breveley came to pick up Simon. Claudette was to accompany the little boy, and look after him in his convalescence. She said goodbye to

Claire, and they both promised to keep in touch. Claudette warmly invited her friend to visit her in her small apartment whenever she came to Paris. Shortly after Claudette had left the room, Simon's father came in.

Claire sensed that his attitude toward her had changed. Before, he had been kind, but coolly professional, and she had felt intimidated by him. Now, his eyes had a softer expression. He stood close to the side of the bed and spoke quietly, in a voice charged with emotion.

"My dear Claire, I shall never be able to find a way to thank you enough for what you have done. Your courage, your real heroism, saved my son's life. I must leave now, but I'll be seeing you again very soon, and then I'll try to express my gratitude and affection a bit better."

Claire answered him quite candidly. "I love Simon very much, Dr. Breveley. There's no need for you to thank me. It . . . it was an easy decision to make."

"Au revoir, then, Claire. . . . You are a very courageous young woman." He took both her hands in his and pressed them warmly for a moment, then turned and left the room. In spite of an overall feeling of contentment, a number of things were still bothering her.

While she was trying to sort out her thoughts the nurse came into the room, and said, "Miss de Montebourg, someone is here to see you. Do you feel well enough to receive a visitor?"

Claire was intrigued. Who could it be? Her heartbeat quickened—Dave? No, it couldn't be Dave so soon. She glanced in the mirror and quickly tidied her hair.

"Yes, I feel fine."

The door opened and Claire's stepmother, Elaine, stalked in, wearing a very elegantly cut black suit. Almost in shock, Claire was speechless, choked by an inexplicable anguish.

"Hello, Claire," said Elaine, her tone cool and refined. "I see that you've fully recovered."

"But . . . how did you know I was here?"

"You've become something of a celebrity, my dear. You made headlines in one of the Paris newspapers," Elaine replied dryly, tapping a copy of the paper beside her purse.

She sat down next to the bed and gazed at Claire coolly. There was an awkward pause.

"How is father?" asked Claire timidly.

Elaine's stare became glacial.

"Please, answer me," insisted Claire, suddenly feeling alarmed. "He isn't ill? Oh!"

She had just realized that Elaine was dressed in black from head to foot, and was wearing no jewelry.

"He died last week. I assumed you knew."

Claire's face was white. Stunned, she closed her eyes. "How could I have known? This is unbelievable! Father! He was never sick! It . . . was it an accident?"

She made no effort to hide the tears that began to run down her cheeks.

"It seems to me," said Elaine, "that you have never been very concerned about anything that might have happened to your father. Forgive me if I find this sudden display of grief a little false. You might as well put an end to this little drama; I know you far too well to believe it. Yes, your father was suffering from a fatal disease, but no one knew about it . . . least of all, me," she added, caustically.

Perhaps her stepmother was really suffering,

thought Claire. Surely, their mutual bereavement could bring them closer together at last. She took Elaine's hand in hers. "This must have been very difficult for you. I know that there have been times in the past when I was very thoughtless, and I ask you to forgive me for any trouble I might have caused you."

Claire was weeping openly. "Did father ask for me before he died? Oh, I'll never forgive myself for not being at his side."

Elaine pulled her hands away. Her eyes were flashing as she got to her feet. "Oh, stop it, Claire. This emotion is much too late and not at all sincere. Yes, your father asked for you. In fact, he wrote this letter to you."

Elaine drew an envelope from her purse and threw it disdainfully onto the bed. She paused, looking down her thin nose at Claire, her supercilious expression never changing.

"Well, you've got that, anyway." Elaine's long red fingernail flicked contemptuously at the white envelope lying on the hospital bedspread. "His last thoughts were of you. Even during those final moments, you came between us, just as you did so many times before. I had no choice but to accept it, without a word. Oh, you cannot imagine how much I hated you! I hated you then, and I hate you now!"

Elaine was breathing quickly, and opened her mouth to say more, but then obviously decided against it.

Claire was completely distraught. She was horrified at the invective coming from her stepmother.

Then Elaine continued, "The newspapers and the radio have been going on and on, acclaiming your exploit. That kind of publicity is in the poorest of taste, and it's got to stop. From now on, I forbid you to use the name de Montebourg."

"But that's my name! I've never done anything to bring dishonor to it!" Claire gasped, hurt to the core. "And surely you're exaggerating about the publicity. . . ."

Elaine's eyes shone with malice. "Have you forgotten the conversation you were supposed to have with my husband on Christmas Eve?" she asked, ignoring Claire's last remark. "Your telegram led us to believe that you were already aware of what the conversation was going to be about, but perhaps not!"

Elaine articulated her next words carefully, for full effect. "You are not the daughter of the Count and Countess de Montebourg! Poor deluded Claire! They simply took you in when you were about three weeks old. No one ever knew. The count was permitted to add his name to yours on the civil registry in the small Swiss village where you were born, but there was never any legal adoption. Before he died, my husband turned over all the relevant documents to his lawyers. On several occasions, a lawyer from the firm tried to get in touch with you at your place of employment, but without success."

Claire felt the ground shift beneath her. She was sure she was going to suffocate.

I MUSTN'T FAINT IN FRONT OF ELAINE, she thought, desperately hanging on to her fast-disappearing consciousness. With incredible effort, she managed to speak.

"Who . . . were my parents?"

"No one of any importance," replied Elaine, shrugging. "They were an ordinary couple who lived near

Interlaken. The count had known them during his travels in Switzerland. Your mother died when you were born. Your father, a mountain guide, was killed soon after in a climbing accident. The count's first wife, in her insanity, decided that you'd been sent to her from heaven, and my husband was such a soft man that he took you in and raised you as his own daughter."

Her hand was on the doorknob as she spoke these last few words and she waited, hoping to see Claire's reaction. But Claire was in a state of shock, dazed by what she'd just been told, and incapable of making the slightest gesture.

The door slammed and Claire was alone.

Some minutes later, Claire's fumbling, restless hands touched paper, and she picked up the envelope from the count, turning it over and over in her fingers.

Moving in slow motion, she slit the envelope roughly with her forefinger, half ripping it. Then she unfolded the single sheet it contained. She read the beautifully scripted paragraphs twice, with growing wonderment.

My dearest daughter,
Although I know that you know the truth about yourself now, you are still my dearest daughter, and always have been. I am fully and painfully aware, now that it's too late, that I have done nothing to make you think of me as your loving father.

I have just discovered that the pain I've been feeling for some time now will shortly be the end of me—so say the best-known doctors in the land.

How can I possibly hope to convince you of my

love for you? I can't, of course, but somehow I have to try.

When you were a little girl, we were a perfectly contented family, never dreaming that our happiness would end so abruptly. Then, as you know, your mother died. I say your mother, and not your adoptive mother, because she was your real mother, in all but actual birth-ties. She and I both adored you. She had started to have incredible headaches some months before she died, and it had changed her. Her mind started to go, and one evening she wandered off on her own, and was finally found, the next morning, in the pond on the grounds.

When she died, a large part of what had been me died with her. She had taught me what loving and giving really meant, but somehow, when she went, she took those gifts with her.

The rest you know. I wanted so much to respond to your obvious love and affection, and to show you how proud I was at all you accomplished, but I couldn't.

I love you, little Claire. Goodbye.

Claire spent a sleepless night. If only she and the count had been able to communicate their love for one another while he was still alive! She knew that the pain would pass, in time, but there would always be a scar on her heart.

She realized how vain it had been for her to be so proud of being a de Montebourg. All this time, her birth certificate had shown the name Claire Frugen de Montebourg. Her parents must have been called Frugen. "No one of any importance," Elaine had said, but that merely revealed the extent of her own incredible snobbishness. Claire's parents had probably been as good and as kind as nanny.

After some hours of tossing and turning in the darkness, a sense of deliverance started to well up from her subconscious. If no de Montebourg blood flowed in her veins, then neither was she subject to the hereditary madness that ran in the family! Elaine's revelations finally had broken the chains of terror that her imagination had forged. But Claire was too hurt and shocked to be able to rejoice. At length she fell into an exhausted sleep.

When Claire awoke the next morning, she found Dave sitting in the chair beside her bed, his dark eyes fixed on her face. Wordlessly, she stretched out her arms and he immediately sprang up and folded her in a crushing embrace.

"Claire . . . Claire . . ." he kept repeating, whispering the words, his face buried in her hair. "Claire, last night I came to see you. . . . You looked so pale. You'd been improving and regaining your strength and color so quickly . . . what happened? I was so worried . . . I couldn't find out anything from the nurse . . . were you upset?" Words tumbled from Dave's lips as he looked at her searchingly . . . lovingly.

Claire listened to the love in Dave's voice and looked at the love in his face. "It doesn't matter, now, what happened. It's over," she said simply. "I learned a few . . . home truths, last night, that's all."

Dave returned to the chair, but leaned forward, taking both of her hands in his. "I learned something last night, too, Claire. I learned that it's important to tell someone you love them—to admit the love to yourself first—then share it with the other person. I love you, Claire. I probably did right from the beginning, but I guess it's taken until now to realize it. Claire, please marry me."

Blinded by tears, her voice choked with emotion, Claire finally managed to answer. "I love you, too, Dave . . . with all my heart. But there's something you should know: I'm really not who you think I am. . . ."

"I believe I ought to propose to you more formally," interrupted Dave with mock solemnity. "Miss Claire Frugen, will you do me the honor of becoming my wife?"

Claire's mouth was trembling. She gazed up at Dave, then stammered, "How did you know my real name?"

"I told him," said a voice from behind them.

Anne-Marie walked into the hospital room, dressed in her best velvet dress. There was a broad smile on her face. "Dave came to me in a panic," she explained placidly. "He was afraid of the fever you had gotten after that horrendous flight from the island, and he wanted to know whether you were strong . . . whether you'd been healthy as a little girl. I told him you'd always been a very resilient little thing, and that you'd pull out of this fever just fine. I told him you were the product of hardy mountain people."

"But if you've known the truth all along," wailed Claire, "why didn't you ever tell me?"

"I didn't know myself until last week, when I received a letter from the countess. I had read about the count's death in the paper—oh, Claire, I'm so terribly sorry, dear," Anne-Marie said sympathetically, realizing Claire's shock at the news. "I know how much you loved him; how terrible for you to have found out this way. I did send you a letter, dear, but you obviously didn't get it. The mail must have been held up by the storm."

"Go on, nanny," Claire said quietly. "What does my father's death have to do with you finding out about my . . . origins?"

"Well, dear, I sent a note of condolence to your stepmother, the countess. She wrote back to me to thank me for my letter and then launched into a long explanation of how you'd been taken in as a baby by the count and his first wife. My, what a hateful letter it was . . . so full of spite and malice.

"Now, I think I'll got out and try to find a cup of tea somewhere; I could use one." Anne-Marie came over to plant a kiss on Claire's cheek, then tactfully took her leave.

"I don't believe, my dear Miss Frugen, that I ever got an answer to my proposal," Dave said mockingly, but before Claire had a chance to reply, his mouth was on hers.